THE STOLEN GIRLS

A DI SCOTT BAKER CRIME THRILLER

JAY NADAL

INKUBATOR
BOOKS

Published by Inkubator Books
www.inkubatorbooks.com

ISBN (eBook): 978-1-83756-042-4
ISBN (Paperback): 978-1-83756-043-1
ISBN (Hardcover): 978-1-83756-044-8

Previously published by the author as Stolen.

PROLOGUE

Loud banging from downstairs broke the stillness of the night. For a moment Renshaw wasn't sure if he was still dreaming or in a parallel state of semiconsciousness. He tried hard to ignore the noise, hoping it would leave him in peace.

He wanted to be left alone to indulge in his thoughts of the pole dancer from last night and the private dance she'd given him in the booth, memories that aroused him once again.

More banging occurred, this time on the door. Drunken youths were no doubt the culprits, eager to grab another drink to fuel their rampant aggression.

"Will you fuck off..." Renshaw groaned in frustration from under his covers, hoping the noise would stop if he ignored it.

Antisocial behaviour was common in this area. Night after night, discarded food wrappers would tumble over each other as the light breeze tossed them around. Salad and kebab meat would litter the pavement. The stale stench of urine and vomit would hit you from closed doorways –

evidence of the lowlifes who hung around his neighbourhood.

The repetitive banging turned into a thundering, wall-vibrating commotion. He startled fully awake, heart racing, pulse vibrating in his ears. An orchestra of sound swirled around his head as his panic grew. Seconds later, what sounded like the front door of the Unicorn pub flying off its hinges sent shock waves through him.

Fully alert and in the pitch dark, he tried hard to focus on who or what might be coming.

Waves of fear rippled through his sweaty body when Renshaw heard someone moving downstairs.

Who is it? What do they want?

His attempt to breathe quietly sounded like a panting dog.

He crept across the bedroom, one foot in front of the other, desperate to avoid squeaky floorboards that would give his position away.

More noise. It sounded like chairs being moved around downstairs. He had two choices: call the police or confront the toerag. But in reality, he knew he had only one option.

Renshaw took a few deep breaths at the top of the stairs and peered into the dark murkiness. The breaths did not calm him on this occasion.

It was now or never.

The switch he flicked on flooded the stairs and hallway with an incandescent glow. It stopped the sounds. He took one step at a time, saying nothing, hoping that the lack of response from him might unnerve the scrote.

A thought crossed his mind. *If there's more than one, then I'm proper fucked. Shit, I left my baseball bat upstairs. Idiot. Too late to go back up now.*

Walking through the doorway, the light in the hallway silhouetted his frame. Ahead, in the unlit room, he could just make out a large dark figure standing in the middle of the space. The intruder didn't flinch or say a word. A tense stand-off added to the knots of worry twisting deep within him. His stomach churned; his bowels quivered and loosened as he stood there.

"What the fuck do you want, you wanker?" he shouted, eyes narrowing to focus in the darkness. He hoped his aggressive choice of words might deter the intruder.

Still no answer came from the dark stranger, who didn't move.

His body tensed when he was set upon from both sides. Two further intruders each grabbed an arm. Their vice-like grip sent shooting pains through his arms. His hands tingled as the tourniquet-like pressure cut off his blood supply.

Renshaw protested again, his efforts futile as he tried to dislodge their grip, twisting his body to escape his human chains. He looked around him in a desperate attempt to see more, hoping to recognise the brutes holding him. But he saw little. Only a cold faint glow from the hall revealed shadows around the room.

Panic coursed through him when a hood covered his head, robbing him of any visual his eyes had to work with.

What's happening? Who are these people? Am I going to die?

Sporadic thoughts tumbled through his mind whilst waves of nausea threatened to erupt like a spewing volcano.

His attackers dragged him into the centre of the room, his bare feet catching on the rough carpet. He let out a sharp scream when his toes collided with the table and chairs. Renshaw listened hard for even the slightest of words, a clue to the accents, even a name, but nothing came.

Of course there'd be nothing. These men had been planning this for a few weeks, each member no doubt aware of their role and duty tonight.

The men dumped him unceremoniously into a chair; he

groaned from their rough treatment. They tied his arms forcibly behind the back of the chair, leaving him defenceless. Unsure of his fate, his eyes welled up; the first of many tears streamed down his cheeks, the saltiness mixing with his saliva as he breathed rapidly.

"Who are you?" Renshaw shouted. "What do you want? Take the money." His questions were met with a hard fist to the jaw.

The impact disorientated him. At first, he felt nothing, but the shock was soon replaced with a stinging sensation around his mouth. He had little time to recover before the second blow connected. The punch sent his mind and consciousness into a spin.

The next few moments seemed to last forever as punches and kicks rained down on his body from every angle. His body protested to the pain shooting through it. His arms stung as the men used a solid instrument to beat him. It was hard to tell what part of him hurt the most.

The assault lasted just a minute or so but long enough to render him semiconscious. His arms were finally cut loose, but the stiffness kept him rooted to the spot. He soon toppled to one side, his body unable to support him; the floor gave him the final blow.

At least he was still alive, for that he was grateful, but he'd underestimated them.

With the hood still in place, one of the men kicked him so hard, it winded him. Renshaw coughed and gasped, air expelling from his lungs quicker than he could breathe it in. Panic gripped him; sweat clung his T-shirt tightly to his back; his eyes stung as he blinked furiously.

"Please leave me alone now," he groaned.

His stomach ached, the muscles in spasm, as they contracted to shield his vital organs from the assault. More hits came as he endured another attack from all sides. The hardness of boot tips buried themselves deep into his flesh.

At least they have left my face alone. That was some blessing.

More burning pain enveloped his body as more hits were delivered. His muscles screamed in agony – he'd never experienced anything like it before.

The hits stopped, and Renshaw lay there slipping in and out of consciousness. Saliva dripped from his mouth. All around him, he heard bottles being smashed, mirrors being broken into a thousand pieces, tables being thrown against the wall.

The silence returned as the men's footsteps faded into the distance.

The pub had been left as broken as his body.

1

It was one of those rare occasions when Detective Inspector Scott Baker was the last to arrive at a crime scene.

He stood at the edge of the car park in Madeira Drive, looking out over the beach and beyond. Scott noticed a calmness to the sea, marred only by a hive of police activity around a small white forensic tent near the water's edge.

His shoes sank into the stony sand as he traipsed across the beach to the scene, a cold slice of toast in one hand, his piping hot coffee in the other. He was grateful that at least some of his breakfast had remained warm.

As he approached the police cordon, Scott paused for a moment to scan the scene. They had found a body close to the shore, in a secluded spot on the beach.

Madeira Drive ended at the car park where he'd just left his car. It was unlikely that much traffic came down this far. There would probably be the odd articulated lorry parked up for a rest stop. He looked beyond the road to a shallow incline of grass that stretched as far as Marine Parade, the main coast road heading out of Brighton towards Rottingdean.

He turned his attention back to the beach that stopped two hundred yards farther up where it hit the marina wall. From where he stood, he knew there weren't many opportunities for witnesses, due to the lack of vantage points. Drawing from his own experiences, he knew a few hardened runners would run along the drive and then back up on to Marine Parade. The busy flow of traffic along the main road would be oblivious to the gruesome attack on the beach.

PC Willits was the scene guard today. It had been a while since he'd last seen her on a previous case involving the murder of Edward Stone, and on that occasion, he'd been off with her. He was determined to make amends.

She greeted him as if nothing had happened. "Morning, sir."

"Morning," he replied with a smile. He fumbled for a moment, struggling to hold his toast and coffee. He looked around for somewhere to dispose of the remnants of his breakfast before getting kitted up. In frustration, he tossed the last piece of toast a few feet away.

A few eager seagulls floating on the thermals swooped down. They squawked and bickered amongst themselves as they fought for their prize until one triumphant victor emerged, scooping it up and making its escape.

"Crikey, these buggers are getting bigger and bigger," he commented. He saw seagulls as nothing more than oversized pigeons, but now that he was up close and personal, it felt like they were the size of bloody albatrosses.

Scott thrust his mug towards the PC, forcing her to grab it hastily. After signing her scene log, he dressed himself in a protective suit and overshoes before retrieving his cup and disappearing through the cordon.

DS Abby Trent and DC Mike Wilson were on the scene, huddled together and comparing notes. Abby looked up when he approached.

"What have we got, Abby?" Scott enquired, sipping on the last dregs of his coffee as he continued to walk past them and to the forensics tent. Abby joined him to brief him en route.

"We've got a young girl in there, and she's known to us, guv. I remember her. I cautioned her about four months ago for soliciting."

"And now she's dead," Scott said, shaking his head as he entered the tent. Seeing a dead body proved challenging at the best of times, especially crime scenes involving children. Most officers felt the same. It was a natural human response. For those officers who had children, or in his case had had a child, it was particularly distressing.

"Hey you." His thoughts were broken by the warm greeting from Cara Hall. The pathologist was on her knees inside the tent, inspecting the victim's arms. "You took your time getting here, Detective. You're normally the first in the queue," she said with a mischievous grin.

"Well, you know me, Cara – I like to mix it up, keep people on their toes," he fired back with a wink. "Thanks for bringing it up though. It's nice to know you're so vigilant about my comings and goings."

"You'd be surprised just how much I remember about you from the catch-up we had, Scott Baker," she replied.

"Now you're scaring me." He enjoyed Cara's dry humour. Scott reflected on how Cara had already brought some lightness in to his life. After all, she'd made him smile again. He'd struggled for so long to come to terms with his loss and disconnect from the cloud of misery that darkened every day. Though a part of him continued to grieve, Cara had thrown him a lifeline that he wanted to reach out and grab with both hands.

Their eyes locked for a few seconds longer than needed, a fact that didn't go unnoticed by Abby.

He cleared his throat. “What can you tell us so far?” Scott asked as he crouched beside the victim and Cara.

“We’re dealing with a young victim. She hasn’t been in the water longer than twelve hours.” Pointing to the puncture marks in the fold of her arm, Cara remarked, “We have marks on both arms and behind the knees. Other than a compression to the side of her head, there are no other visible signs as to cause of death. I’ll know more when I open her up. She does have extensive bruising to her face, arms and legs, though.” Cara sighed and stood.

“She’s missing all her fingernails too,” she added.

2

Scott looked at the bloodied mess that once were the girl's fingernails. "If it had been one fingernail, it could have been accidental, but to have all ten missing..."

Cara nodded. She placed plastic bags over the girl's hands to preserve any evidence. "There's lots of tissue damage around the nail bed and cuticle. I'll look in closer detail when I examine her. We'll remove her from the scene once forensics have done their thing."

The girl was no older than fifteen or sixteen but dressed to look older. Her shoulder-length, mousy brown hair was tangled and matted with seaweed. She was still clothed in a black blouse and black skirt, together with black knee-length boots.

Scott studied her thin frame, hollow cheeks and sunken eyes, evidence of drug abuse, working the streets and poor nutrition. He struggled to comprehend how a child's youth could be stolen, her mind and body exploited by the same people who should be protecting her, her journey to adulthood corrupted and short-lived. It preyed on his mind. He only wished he could do more to stamp out this cruel industry that preyed on the vulnerable.

"For fuck's sake," he said through gritted teeth. His outburst took both Abby and Cara by surprise.

Scott looked at Abby briefly; they shared a silent moment of anger and despair. Abby's only response was a very slight shake of her head.

Cara placed one hand on his shoulder and gave it a gentle squeeze. "You okay, Scott?"

"Yes, I'm fine. Stuff like this just sickens me." He stood, his knees cracking as he straightened up. "What time is the post-mortem?"

"She'll be the second one today; she's ready for moving if forensics are done – the longer we're here, the more attention we'll attract. I'd imagine noon. Does that work for you?"

"Sounds good to me. I'll see you there."

Abby and Scott stepped outside the tent. He took a big lungful of fresh air to clear his head.

"Scott and Cara, hey, first-name terms, then?" Abby said with a smile. "You care to spill the beans?"

"I'm on first-name terms with lots of people. There's Matt in forensics. I call you Abby. I even call Sheila the tea lady, Sheila." Scott changed the subject. "What do we know about the victim?"

"Her name is Libby Stevens; she's fifteen. I nicked her and gave her a caution for soliciting about four months ago. Her popular patches were around Kemp Town and around the back of the station. I tried to get her help at the time, but she wasn't having any of it. She looked terrified when I nicked her. I just wish I could have done more."

"I know," Scott agreed. "We can't be expected to help everybody who comes through here. We're juggling umpteen daily cases; we don't have the time to set everyone straight. Get Sian and Raj to have a wander round. They should get a statement from the jogger who found her. I can't see many CCTV cameras. The nearest one appears to be over there." Scott waved at the marina wall. "We can always try there, but I won't hold my breath. There's also the David Lloyd gym and the casino just over the other side of the marina wall. They may have some cameras that could have picked up something."

"Will do, guv. Anything else?"

"Not for now. I'll head to the PM. Meet me there at one. Later this afternoon we'll have a full team debrief."

"Thought the PM was at twelve?" Abby questioned.

"It is," Scott confirmed. "But we don't need to attend unless it's necessary." He hated autopsies.

Abby didn't reply; he could see she was pondering what lay ahead this afternoon. As a parent, she likely felt a sympathetic twinge for the loss of a child so young. The deceased girl was the same age as her own daughter, Sophie.

The contrast between the two young girls' lives couldn't be more different. Sophie was still at school, battling with the things that most girls of her age had to contend with: spots, hormones and boys. Libby had been thrust into the cruel and seedy world of drugs, exploitation, prostitution and abandonment.

Scott doubted if Libby had known what it was like to celebrate a birthday with family, or bicker with siblings, or even have a hug from a parent who loved her.

It's a cruel world we live in.

"I want to pull out all the stops for this case. We owe it to Libby to find out what happened to her." Scott reflected on the situation with a gentle nod of his head.

Any loss of life was sad, and Scott had faced his own

demons. Losing his own child had hurt him more than he cared to admit. To witness another young life destroyed tied his stomach up in knots.

Scott looked back at the forensics tent, hands clenched into fists. He would get justice one way or another.

3

The post-mortem was in its advanced stages when Scott and Abby arrived at the mortuary. They put on protective gowns before entering the main examination area.

"These places always give me the heebie-jeebies," Abby remarked as they walked past two tables that had two bodies cloaked beneath paper shrouds.

Abby whispered, "I remember reading a newspaper article. Apparently, a mortuary worker in Ghana used to have sex with dead bodies because he couldn't get living women to date him."

Scott turned to her, rolling his eyes and shaking his head. "And you believe everything you read in the paper?"

Abby shrugged. "It's true."

"Scotty." Cara's eyes lit up as she saw him approaching. Abby raised an eyebrow in Scott's direction.

He cleared his throat in embarrassment. "Afternoon, Cara. I brought a second set of eyes with me." He flipped his hand in Abby's direction.

Cara greeted her with a warm nod.

The sight of Libby Stevens naked on the table was in marked contrast to the way they had seen her just a few hours ago. Back on the beach, despite her being dead, she still looked normal – or as normal as she could look. But here now, she was nothing more than a body being taken apart in the name of forensics, to determine the cause of death. Both Scott and Abby paused as they stood by her. A heady mix of consternation, sadness and revulsion washed over him.

Scott scanned her body first but was taken aback as he looked at her face. The scalp had been cut and peeled back to cover the front of her head. The top section of her skull and brain had been removed for analysis.

"Poor girl," Abby said quietly with a heavy breath.

She and Scott exchanged glances, their eyes reflecting similar angst.

Scott assessed more of the girl's body; her rib cage had been removed, and her inner organs taken for weighing and analysis. All that remained now was an empty red cavern that was now a perfect receptacle to catch bodily fluids. A mortuary technician was using what looked like a soup ladle to spoon out the collected fluid.

What caught Scott's attention was the extensive tissue damage where the girl's vagina used to be. This caused Scott to wince in disgust.

"You want to give us the short story, Cara?" he asked.

"Well, it's the early stages of the post-mortem, and she's in a bad way, so I'll be here for a few more hours. I've taken samples and sent them to toxicology. We should have them back tomorrow. She has a tattoo on her left ankle, with the word 'love' written inside a heart. The missing fingernails were removed deliberately. Under the magnifier, there appears to be lacerations around the nail bed and cuticle, which suggests that they were pulled out."

Scott nodded. "As you thought earlier."

She nodded in agreement.

Cara continued, "There's limited wrinkling to her skin, in particular on the palms of her hands and the soles of her feet. This suggests to me that she wasn't in the water for long. Had she been in longer, you would be seeing significant loosening of the skin and separation of the skin on her fingers. She didn't drown either. Her lungs aren't waterlogged, and by that I mean there's no water in the lungs, and there's no frothy fluid in her airways."

Cara continued her analysis as she scanned the cadaver. "She was a smoker, with early discolouration to the lungs. She has eleven puncture marks in total on her arms and behind her knees, conducive with injecting. There is localised tissue damage to her veins as a result. There's a small amount of skin and soft-tissue damage around her face and legs. Likely causes are marine animals or fish feeding off her, I'm afraid." Cara moved around the table. "We also have general injuries and abrasions to her face and legs, more than likely caused by intermittent contact with the seabed or other hard structures." She sighed, her eyes flitting between Scott and Abby. "However, that's not the worst."

Scott and Abby exchanged a look of knowing as they prepared themselves for what was about to come next.

"Does it get any worse?" Abby asked, her eyes narrowing as she crossed her arms protectively around her body. Her face blanched. Abby grabbed Scott's arm to steady herself.

"You want to leave?" Scott offered. He too was suffering but handling it slightly better.

Abby shook her head. "No, I'll be fine."

4

Cara continued, "She's had her tongue cut out. The stub suggests it wasn't a very clean cut. But there wasn't much trauma inside her mouth. I would suggest that she didn't put up any resistance."

"Hold on a minute," Scott interrupted, closing his eyes for a moment. "Back up a sec. Are you suggesting that she was already dead prior to having it removed?"

Cara nodded. "Most likely. Had she been alive when they'd removed her tongue, there would be lacerations inside her mouth, simply due to the small space in which they were working and the potential struggle she would have put up."

Abby sighed, shaking her head. "I don't think I need to hear any more."

"I'm afraid you do," Cara urged.

Pointing at the victim's genital area, Cara leant over it in a macabre way, to get a closer look. "She's got extensive external and internal injuries. I examined her from the outside and through her lower abdomen cavity, and the damage extends far inside her. In my opinion, the injuries are consistent with the use of a blunt instrument that was forcibly used to penetrate her."

Abby was visibly shaken. She wiped her eyes with the back of her hand.

Scott's heart beat faster due to a combination of shock and anger that forced him to tense up. His stomach churned; his jaw muscles tensed as he gritted his teeth. With a deep breath, he straightened and pulled his shoulders back. Scott massaged his forehead with his fingers, beginning to comprehend the final savage moments in this girl's life.

"The sick bastard, someone really had it in for her, didn't they? Any indication of the actual cause of death?"

Cara nodded. "Hypovolaemic shock, also known as haemorrhagic shock, is my initial conclusion."

"And what is that in English?" Abby asked.

"I believe she bled to death. It happens when you lose more than twenty per cent of your body's blood or fluid supply. This severe fluid loss makes it impossible for the heart to pump a sufficient amount of blood around your body, and it leads to systemic organ failure. Bleeding from blunt trauma injuries as well as internal bleeding can lead to this."

Scott frowned. Abby had a similar bemused look.

Cara tried a different approach. "Okay, let me explain it to you in layman's terms. As your heart begins to shut down and fails to circulate enough blood through your body, the symptoms of shock occur. Blood pressure plummets, and there's a severe drop in body temperature, which can be life threatening. She didn't get medical attention and died as a result."

"She died a slow, painful death, and we're looking for a sick murderer." Revulsion coursed through Scott and chilled his body.

When I get my hands on this sick fucker... Just me and him in a room. With the door locked and my warrant card left outside.

He worked hard to control his breathing and remain objective. "Okay, thanks, Cara. We'll leave you to carry on so we can get back to the office."

"Sure thing, Scotty. Sorry it's a bad one for you guys." She smiled sympathetically. "Give me a shout later if you've got time for a slice of cake and a cuppa. My treat."

"Seriously, Cara, how can you talk about food when you've got this in front of you?" Scott shook his head in startled disbelief. "You don't need cake because you're already a fruitcake."

Her ability to be unfazed by her work perplexed him.

Cara just shrugged and smiled as she watched them leave.

5

Scott and Abby drove back to the station in silence to begin with, both taking the needed time to reflect on Libby's cause of death.

Abby broke the silence. "Slice of cake and a cuppa? Really?"

"And what's wrong with that?" Scott challenged.

"Hardly subtle, is she? She wants you as dessert." Abby teased him, turning in her seat to face him. "I think she's got a soft spot for you."

"You're just jealous."

"I am. I wish I had a fella chasing me like that." Abby returned to gaze out the passenger window.

"Well, you need to get yourself out there, then, don't you? Before you turn old and wrinkly," he teased back.

Abby turned back in horror. "Oi! I'm not past my sell-by date yet." She sighed. "I wish I could, but truth be told, I'm a bit scared really. The thought of starting all over again with someone new..." She paused for a moment. "Been there, done that, bought the T-shirt. It's the hassle of when things don't work out that bothers me. I don't want to introduce the kids to a parade of men."

Scott burst out laughing whilst trying to drive in a straight line. "Parade of men? Fancy your chances at pulling *all* the single men in Brighton, do you?"

Abby laughed, trying to backtrack. "One would be nice, but I won't hold my breath. I just attract the weirdos, halitosis sufferers, and those who want me to handcuff them to the bed for some kinky fun."

Scott nodded slowly, amused by her observations. "That's what I like about you, Abby, always a glass-half-full person."

SCOTT GATHERED with his team around the briefing table.

"Right, we need to know the who, the why and the when around this case." There were collective nods from his team.

"Abby, for the benefit of the others, what can you tell us about Libby Stevens?"

Abby glanced around the table as she cleared her throat. "I cautioned Libby for soliciting a few months ago. She was picking up punters from outside the Unicorn pub in Fleet Street, which is around the back of the train station. She'd take them to either the car park in Stroudley Road or the waste ground next door, to do her tricks. If she got lucky with a rich punter, then she'd go to the Jury's Inn. It was all about the money at the time, getting it as quick as she could to feed her habit. She wanted in and out, if you pardon the expression."

A slip like that would normally have been met with derisive laughter, but there was a sombre mood to this briefing.

"Anything else?" Scott asked.

"Yes. Just before that, she was knocking about with a boyfriend by the name of Johnny Wright. Uniform had a few words with the pair for loitering around the shops. They chased them out of the Churchill Square shopping centre for potential shoplifting."

Scott nodded. "Okay, thanks, Abby. There's not much to go on at the moment. The post-mortem is underway, so we should get the full report tomorrow. However, I do want to point out that Libby Stevens" – he turned to her picture on the whiteboard – "was subjected to a violent sexual assault. She also had all her fingernails pulled out, and her tongue was removed. The poor girl bled to death. I'd like to say that she died quickly and suffered little pain, but evidence suggests otherwise."

"We're dealing with a real sick individual here, guv," said Mike. "I was talking to the forensic team on scene, and they weren't that optimistic about getting much evidence. She'd spent too long in the water. Any usable evidence may have washed off."

Scott looked around the room. "What else have we got?"

DC Raj Singh shuffled his papers and sat upright. "Nothing on the CCTV front, guv. There are two CCTV cameras at opposite ends of the marina wall. They focus on the main access road behind the David Lloyd club and the casino. There's nothing looking over the crime scene. But just in case, I asked for a copy of the recordings for the past twenty-four hours."

"Good thinking. Okay, we need to start doing some digging. Her ex-boyfriend Johnny is a good place to start. Abby and I will go and see him first thing in the morning. Sian and Mike, I want you both to speak to the local drug users in and around town, and in particular up near the train station. See if any of them came into contact with Libby. Find out who the suppliers are too. Can you check for other prostitutes in the same vicinity? Some may have known Libby. See if any of them had clients who were a little rough with them."

"You reckon it could be a punter?" DC Sian Mason asked.

"It's certainly a worthwhile line of enquiry," Scott said. "We can't rule anything out at the moment."

He walked over to the window and leant against the windowsill, facing the room. His right hand was in his pocket; he tapped a pen on the windowsill with his left hand.

Trying to formulate a plan, Scott stared at the sunlight bouncing off the table. "Raj, contact social services and see what they've got on Libby Stevens. If she is fifteen, then she must have been in a foster home or residential care unit. Let's see if they can shed some light on her situation and background."

Raj nodded.

"Any other questions?" Scott asked as he searched the faces of his team. Each of them was quieter than normal. "Listen up. I know this case is going to be hard. If this morning is anything to go by, we're in for a rough ride. Abby and I both found the PM hard. My door is always open. If anything becomes too much for you, pop in and let's have a chat, okay?"

There were appreciative nods from his team.

Scott continued, "Well then, let's crack on. Let's find out what happened to this girl."

6

The address Scott and Abby were visiting the next morning was in the up-and-coming New England Quarter of Brighton. It was a part of a regeneration project consisting of stylish, tall, white and brown buildings housing trendy, affordable flats, town houses and homes. It was built on the largest brownfield site in Brighton.

The area was steeped in history. The site sat adjacent to the railway station and had once consisted of high-density housing from a bygone era. It had suited those who worked on the railways and the goods yards that serviced the station.

By the mid-1900s, the area had seen a rapid decline after those very same yards and factories closed down. The site had been cleared and left barren for many years. Discussions, debates and arguments had ensued between various authorities and the community on what should replace it. A few minor projects had been proposed; however, nothing came of them. It soon became an eyesore, hidden behind tall, boarded-up walls – the perfect canvas for local youths to spray murals and tags all over them.

The eyesore had been replaced by a micro-community

within a community, with a mix of hotels, shops, supermarkets and residential facilities.

Scott looked around as they approached the block in question. Despite it being new, modern and clean, he couldn't help but feel that the area was missing something. It didn't feel homely or welcoming. If anything, it was a little cold and soulless. It likely suited the young professionals or small families who needed convenient access to the station and town centre.

On the third floor, a tall, slim, good-looking youth answered the door to flat number twelve. His gelled hair rippled back over his head in waves. He wore a thin, black V-neck jumper and drainpipe jeans. On the face of it, he looked like any other lad Scott would see on the high road.

"Johnny Wright?" he asked.

"Who wants to know?" he asked flippantly.

"I'm Detective Inspector Baker, and this is Detective Sergeant Trent." They briefly waved their warrant cards in front of him. "Can we come in to ask you a few questions?"

Scott didn't wait for a reply as he stepped into the hallway.

"Be my guest." Johnny waved them through sarcastically. "Make yourselves at home, why don't you?"

The flat was bright and airy, with contemporary furniture that gave the impression of comfortable living. To either side of the hallway were doors leading into the bedrooms, one a double and the second no bigger than a box room. The bathroom was a decent enough size with large stone tiles that covered the floor and walls. A large double shower with a waterfall spray head drew Scott's eye, together with the Jack and Jill sinks in white porcelain.

The hallway led to a large room that overlooked the front road. It was tastefully split into a functional kitchen-diner on the right, with white cupboards and black worktops, fitted with sleek, Neff modern appliances. To the left the lounge was minimally kitted out with a luxury leather corner sofa situated directly in front of an oversized, wall-mounted LED TV.

Abby and Scott exchanged an intuitive glance of *this doesn't quite look right*. Either Johnny was in a well-paid job, or he had come into inheritance from a rich old aunt to afford this place. Or he was involved in something illegal.

"Nice place. What do you do for a living?" Scott asked as he continued to look around the room.

"I'm in between jobs at the moment," said Johnny.

Scott nodded slowly. "What *did* you do, then?"

"Erm." The man paused for a second. "I'm self-employed. A bit of DJ'ing, a bit of web design… that sort of thing." He maintained his false bravado and sat down on the sofa, flicking through the Sky channels on TV.

"We want to ask you about Libby Stevens. When did you last see her?" Scott asked.

He smirked. "I guess six months ago. We had a big falling-out, things fizzled out between us, and we moved on." He shrugged. "*C'est la vie*."

A girl walked into the room suddenly, too busy texting on her phone to notice them. Scott's attention shifted to her.

She looked up, visibly tensed, promptly turned, and walked back out into the hallway.

Scott gave the slightest of nods in Abby's direction, which she took as the cue to follow the girl.

7

The hallway floor was covered in natural wood; each of Abby's steps reverberated as she headed to the bedroom.

She peered around the door to see the girl sitting cross-legged on the bed, scrolling through something on an iPad. She was oblivious to Abby's presence until Abby entered the room. The girl scowled at the invasion of privacy. She stared cold-faced and tight-lipped at Abby.

Abby perched on the end of the bed and looked the girl over. She was dressed in a red Superdry T-shirt, and black, three-quarter-length leggings. Her finger- and toenails were painted a deep shiny red. Her thick, long, jet-black hair, which Abby assumed was dyed, hung down her front, partially covering the logo on the front of her top. The darkness of her hair offered a stark contrast to her sparkling, intense blue eyes framed in black eyeliner.

"I'm Detective Sergeant Abby Trent. What's your name?"

"What's it to you?" the girl asked abruptly, still avoiding eye contact.

"Just asking. How old are you, love?"

The girl made no reply. Her fingers moved at lightning speed as she scanned, liked and moved through various Snapchat messages.

"We need to make sure you're all right. What's your name, and how old are you?"

The girl tutted. "Jenna Wade and I'm sixteen."

"And where do you live, Jenna?"

"Why, what's it to you?"

"Well, we perhaps need to check in with your mum to let her know you're okay," Abby suggested.

Jenna showed no signs of softening her attitude towards Abby. She offered the occasional uncooperative glare that most teens had mastered by the time they reached her age. "She won't care anyway."

"All the same, your safety is my concern, Jenna."

Jenna laughed half-heartedly. "I ain't got a mum."

"Dad?"

"You're joking me?"

Abby probed, certain that Jenna was being economical with the truth. "Well then, have you run away? Do you live with an uncle or aunt, foster parents, or even at a residential unit maybe?"

Jenna looked out the window, knowing that to face the officer now would give away too much. Abby had seen it all before. The girl had set and fallen into her own trap, a response that Abby quickly followed up on.

"A residential unit, then? Which one? Tindale, St Mary's, Benedict's?"

"What if I am? I haven't done anything wrong," Jenna insisted.

Abby placed her hand to her chest. "Listen, I'm not saying you have, Jenna. I'm just making sure you're okay and trying to establish some facts." She decided to change tack, to defuse the tense situation a bit. "Did Johnny give you that iPad?"

Jenna smirked, playing with her necklace.

"Did he give you that necklace and bracelet?" Abby added.

Jenna said nothing and placed a protective hand over the bracelet, not wishing to leave it open to more scrutiny.

The girl shifted uncomfortably on the bed, and Abby saw a flash of a familiar tattoo on her left ankle that alarmed her. She'd seen the same design on Libby's left ankle at the post-mortem.

"All the things that Johnny buys you, what does he want in return?"

Jenna exploded. "Why are you asking me? These are stupid questions."

"We're just worried about you."

"I can look after myself. What's with the million questions?"

Abby pulled out a picture of Libby from her handbag and showed it to Jenna. "This is Libby Stevens. Have you seen her, or do you know of her? It's really important."

Jenna's instant reaction told Abby she did. Her eyes widened for just a split second before she composed herself.

Despite the girl's silence, Abby pushed on. "Have you seen her about? This is important."

"I'm not answering your stupid questions," Jenna declared.

"I know, but it would help me if you do. The girl dated Johnny. Did you know that?"

She shrugged. "Big deal, so?"

"He used to give Libby presents too. She even had the same tattoo."

Jenna was looking a little unsure of her footing. "Look, you got it all wrong." Her penetrating blue eyes expressed a mix of joy and sadness. "He's good to me, he looks after me, and he's dead into me. I really love him."

"Ever wonder why he gives you nice things? To impress you? To get something in return maybe?" Abby challenged. "You need to understand that if you're underage and Johnny's sleeping with you, then that's against the law. If you're underage and he's giving you gifts and expecting you to sleep with him in return, then that's coercion and rape."

"No!" Jenna exclaimed, a look of disgust on her face. "It's not like that. You make it sound dirty." She sighed. "Johnny loves me. I know he does."

Abby held up Libby's picture one last time, in an attempt to appeal to the girl's better nature. "You know her, don't you? Please."

Jenna glanced away, giving the slightest of nods. "We saw her two nights ago."

"You and Johnny?"

Jenna nodded. "We saw her outside the Unicorn."

Abby nodded. "Come with me, please."

Jenna got up. Abby walked into the lounge, followed by Jenna sheepishly trailing behind.

Scott was casually flicking through the DVD collection by the front window. He looked up when she entered.

Abby spoke to Johnny. "Why did you lie? Jenna says you saw Libby the night she died. Now I think we deserve an explanation, don't you?"

Scott said nothing as Abby led the questioning.

"We did see her... we didn't stop and chat or anything," Johnny finally admitted.

"Libby's dead. Her body was discovered two days ago."

At hearing the news, Johnny and Jenna shot each other shocked looks. Their bravado deserted them as they sat together on the sofa, looking like two children who'd just been scolded by their mother.

"I'm sorry, I didn't know that," offered Johnny.

Abby's phone started to ring, so she left the room to take it, leaving Scott to carry on.

"What time was that?" she heard Scott ask.

Johnny replied, "Nine thirty. We were off to Xenon's on the seafront."

"We'll check that, so you'd better not be wasting any more of our time."

"Go ahead. We got nothing to hide."

8

"Stroppy pair, aren't they?" Scott concluded as they left the building and stood by the car.

Abby had been great in there. He felt a sense of pride to have Abby on his team; her strong, assertive character was an asset he valued. Her empathetic nature had proved handy on more than one occasion. Letting her loose on Jenna had yielded far better results than he could have achieved with the teenage girl.

"Well, one is certainly stroppy. The other, Jenna, is too vulnerable and impressionable. Something doesn't seem right there, guv." An unease in her voice suggested she was troubled by it. "Until we know more about her, I'm not comfortable leaving Jenna there. If she really is sixteen, then I'm twenty-one."

Scott shared her concerns, but they were treading a fine line between erring on the side of caution and letting things run for another twenty-four hours whilst further investigations were carried out. He hesitated for a moment, weighing up his options. He took a few steps away from the car and studied the ground, his eyes following the many cracks in the pavement.

He turned and walked back to Abby. "Ask Sian to meet you here and then go back in and have another chat with Jenna. Do a risk assessment. We don't know the full facts yet. She didn't look like she was under duress or being held against her will. I couldn't see any signs of physical injury either. Having said that, if she's underage, then she needs to be back in care for her own safety. If necessary, we'll get a police protection order for her until we can confirm her age and circumstances. She won't like it, but that's tough. It's in her best interests."

Abby fumbled around in her handbag for her phone. "That was Sian who called by the way. She and Mike got a lead from one of the street girls. It appears that Libby was hanging around with Simone, a known working girl. She's been done a few times for soliciting. Mike and Sian have just been round to Simone's. Libby had been staying there for about six months but didn't come back on the night in question."

"Six months? About the time Johnny dumped her," Scott added.

"Simone took her under her wing when she found Libby wandering the streets, and one thing led to another. Her addiction needed to be fed, so she started working the streets. Simone went off with a punter the night Libby was killed. But she said that just prior to that, Libby looked upset, scared in fact, and was checking over her shoulder, mumbling things like 'They're coming for me'. Libby was crying, saying she'd seen Johnny and that they'd argued."

"So, matey boy hasn't been completely honest with us."

"Looks like it, guv."

Abby continued, "Simone said that their pimp, Lenny West, was furious with Libby for ripping off clients in the last week or so. She'd get them to pay up front and then run off. He was trying to find her. But here's the interesting part: when Libby was with Johnny, he gave her things. It started with presents, moved on to booze and then ended with drugs."

Scott raised a brow. "She was an addict by the time Simone met her?"

"Yes, looks like it."

"Johnny dumped her, and she started working the streets?"

"No, he didn't dump her, guv; she ran away. She was scared."

"Ran away from what?"

"I don't know, but Lenny might be a good place to start? Guess where he trains every day?"

Scott shrugged. "Go on, surprise me."

"Hardcore gym in Hove... Dave Fraser's old place. Remember that from the previous case?" She tapped the roof of the car with her finger.

He rolled his eyes. "That figures... a den of thieves. Get Mike over there to pick Lenny up for questioning, and I will meet them later at the station."

"Where are you off to?"

"I need to be somewhere."

9

The mild and gentle afternoon sun warmed Scott's shoulders as he knelt next to the plot in Angel's Corner. Three years on and the pain continued to cripple him, a grief that threatened to starve him daily of his breath. Tears filled Scott's eyes and spilled over. His shoulders shook as he cried harder. He tugged hard at his lapel jackets, wanting to scream and release the pain. He felt lost. Emptiness had replaced the life he once had.

Becky's picture stared up at him. Her radiant smile had been captured in a photo taken at her second birthday party with her mother, surrounded by family, friends and toddlers from her playgroup. A simple, heart-shaped stone set in black marble offered a fitting memorial for his daughter's resting place, with the words he'd engraved to reflect her journey: "Too beautiful for Earth."

Becky would have been five now, and oh, how he wished it had been him who'd taken the impact of the car and not Tina and Becky as they crossed the road. She was her mother's daughter all right; they both had long, straight mousy brown hair that cascaded over their shoulders. Both sported matching fringes, and whenever Tina was doing her makeup, Becky would be by her side, delving deep in her makeup drawer. She'd be rummaging around, finding mascaras, eyeliners and lipsticks that she'd crayoned on herself, much to her mother's amusement.

She'd only just come into this world. Becky had so much to look forward to...

"Why... why wasn't it me?" Scott wailed as he looked upwards to the skies. His breathing was heavy and erratic. He fought hard to get control of his emotions, wiping away tears and snot on the sleeve of his jacket.

Seeing Libby had only brought home how fragile life was and how easily another young life had been erased. He had worked hard to control the dark moods and sadness that threatened his happiness. His colleagues were unaware of the turmoil that raged inside him every day. He could handle most anything that life threw at him, but cases that included children were too close for comfort.

He gazed at the photo through red, puffy eyes.

"I miss you, my baby girl. You're my little princess, Daddy's little girl." His voice choked as the words stuck in his throat. "One day we'll be together again. I'm always thinking of you... I'm sorry I let you down. I'm so sorry I couldn't protect you."

As he rose, the magnetic draw to sit there and be with her tormented him. Even in her absence, a part of his life remained there by her stone.

Visiting his daughter was hard, but Scott knew the next stone would be just as painful.

Tina. His wonderful, beautiful wife and mother to his child. He was all cried out, but his body knew the next emotional assault was just moments away.

As he stopped by her grave, he remembered that beautiful, pale blue dress in Tina's picture so well. The first time she'd worn it was on their first wedding anniversary in Tunbridge Wells. They'd enjoyed a romantic meal and evening at a secluded cottage, surrounded by panoramic open spaces and lush green woodland. She'd insisted they make love in the open. The grass was their bed, the moon their illumination.

In that moment, nothing else mattered in the world, just their union, their closeness and love that bonded them as best friends, lovers, soulmates and husband and wife.

Scott's eyes stung from the tears and the incessant rubbing.

His shoulders hung low with grief. He desperately wanted to move on from the tragedy in his life, but the demons of the dark wouldn't let him. They followed him, relishing every opportunity to pull him back into the abyss.

Wiping his eyes for the last time, he drew large lungfuls of air to clear his head before getting back in the car.

As he drove away from Bear Road, he knew it wouldn't be long before he was back here again. Next time he'd bring back a stuffed Peppa Pig toy to keep Becky company.

10

The station was a hive of activity, in marked contrast to the serene setting he'd just left. Scott had stopped off at home for a change of suit and a quick splash of cool water to wash away the sadness that had dried on his face.

When Scott walked into the interview room, Lenny West was slouching casually in the chair with one arm draped over the back. Scott was struck by the man's unusually long neck and large, protruding Adam's apple. West's dark brown hair was unkempt and in need of a wash. A white T-shirt and ripped faded jeans added to his scruffy appearance.

West greeted him with a shrewd smile. His bespectacled solicitor sat po-faced in a grey pinstripe suit and pink tie, looking bored.

After completing the introductions and cautions for the benefit of the recording, Scott took a few silent moments to play a waiting game with West. His solicitor sighed and tapped his pen on the desk in frustration.

Scott finally spoke. "I want to talk to you."

"About what?" West said slowly.

Scott pushed a picture of Libby Stevens across the table.

"Libby Stevens was killed two days ago... Did you know her?" Scott asked, tapping twice on the photo.

West snatched a quick glance before giving Scott his full attention. "Never seen her before." He dismissed the picture with a shrug.

Scott smiled. "That's not what we heard. We heard you were her pimp. Did you supply her with drugs as well?"

"I don't do either. Who put you up to this? Simone?"

"Did you know she was fifteen?" Scott said through gritted teeth.

He hated lowlifes like West. All bravado and no balls. They controlled the vulnerable and weak using intimidation and violence. The law was something they opted into or out of when it suited.

He changed tack. "Never mind... When did you last see Libby? We're interested in her death and the fact that you may have been one of the last people to see her alive. If you're not connected, then it's in your own interest to help us out. Understand?" Scott smiled.

West remained tight-lipped, occasionally looking to his solicitor, who seemed far more interested in the copious notes he was scribbling whilst listening to the exchange.

Scott continued, "Stop wasting my time, West. You were Libby's pimp. A quick trawl of the security cameras from in and around the station will confirm that for us. I'll pull in every one of your girls for a night and hit you where it hurts: your pocket!"

West still hadn't shifted his casual position and appeared nonchalant about the whole escapade. He sighed, as if bored more than anything else. "I saw her briefly. I wanted to tell her to get busy, but she was half-cut, blabbing like a lunatic. Before I could get anywhere near her, she legged it. She was ripping off my customers, and that's not good for business," he summed up and leant back on two legs of the chair.

"Did you give Libby drugs?" Scott narrowed his eyes, weighing up West's version of events.

"No way. Look, I didn't know she was that young, and I never supplied her with any drugs. That's not my scene. I need girls who are with it, if you know what I mean... not looking like they've crawled out of a gutter."

Ironically, that's where you put them, you tosser.

"Who did, then? Libby's ex-boyfriend?" Scott asked. "Although he swears blind that he doesn't touch the stuff and neither did Libby."

West laughed. "And you believed him?" He dropped the chair down and leant forward on the table. "Listen, sometimes Libby used to get angry and mouth off about Johnny. She hated him, said he'd made her an addict just so he could control her."

"How well do you know him? Ever bump into him?"

"Nah, he'd see me and cross the street. Wise kid." West smirked.

"We think he is grooming underage girls for sex. Know anything about that?"

"No. I told you everything I know. She said she was seventeen, nearly eighteen. I had no reason to doubt her. She was a sort, and she kept my punters sweet," he replied with a wink that disgusted Scott. To him she was an asset, not a human being.

"How did you meet Libby?"

"I met her through..." He paused for a moment, looking up from beneath his mop of hair that had fallen over his eyes.

"Simone?"

West nodded. "She was trying to do tricks on Simone's patch. The girls weren't happy. Simone had a soft spot for her and took her in, to help her and show her the ropes. Then she was introduced to me."

"Was she in trouble with anyone else?"

A shake of his head was all that West offered, and Scott concluded the interview not long after.

It left him with little to go on, but it opened up more uncertainty over Libby's last known movements.

One question kept running through his mind: Who had it in for Libby enough to kill her in such a savage manner?

11

The team gathered for an evening briefing. Scott's boss, DCI Harvey, joined them, keen to get a grasp of the current case before the management meeting the following morning.

Raj had brought his usual offering to satisfy his sweet tooth and spoil the team. On this occasion, the officer passed a tray of twelve assorted Krispy Kreme doughnuts around. Sian grabbed one and was greedily devouring hers moments later. Abby, on the other hand, bemoaned the high fat content and complained how far she'd have to run to burn off the calories. It didn't stop her from tucking into a glazed ring one though. Least amount of calories, according to her logic.

DC Mike Wilson, on the other hand, was doing a sterling job of polishing off his custard-filled doughnut in two enormous mouthfuls. Abby shielded her mouth in disgust and looked away.

Scott got the meeting going. "Right, gang, we need to focus on Libby's last known movements. From witness interviews with her pimp and ex-boyfriend, she appeared to be frightened of something or someone. We need to establish what. Any ideas?" He scanned those around the table.

"Disgruntled punter?" Sian asked.

"Possible... However, we also know that her pimp was annoyed about her ripping off customers. She also bumped into her ex on the night she died, and we've found out that she hated him for getting her hooked on drugs. So we have two possible suspects in the frame."

Abby interrupted, "Guv, Johnny used to go to the same school as Libby, so there's a connection there. After he left, he'd hang around outside the school gates, targeting young girls, giving them presents, sweets, fags, etcetera. He's been the subject of calls from concerned parents. Police looked into it. He was cautioned. Nothing more came of it."

Scott nodded. "And the risk assessment?"

"I think we need to get a protection order in place. If Johnny got Libby on drugs, Jenna could be next in line."

"Agreed," said DCI Harvey.

Sian waved a report in the air. "I've got the toxicology report, guv, and there were traces of cocaine in her body."

Scott nodded. "Raj, hit us with where you got with the social."

Raj pulled himself up in his chair, wiping the icing from his mouth on the cuff of his shirt. "Libby was at a residential unit a year ago, St. Benedict's. She ran away from the home to live with Johnny. She was fourteen; he was seventeen. Johnny lavished her with new clothes and trainers, then a new mobile. At first, she was coming home drunk, then not coming home at all, disappearing for days at a time. He'd take her to a youth club a lot, but don't know much about which club, to be honest."

"Did the residential unit inform the police?" Abby asked Raj.

He nodded. "Nothing was done. A young, infatuated girl

ran away with her boyfriend. It's hardly front-page news or a priority. It was reported, but nothing was done about it. It was logged as another missing person report. We have too many MisPer reports and not the resources to follow up on them."

Guilt washed over Scott, and his stomach turned.

Another statistic, perhaps another failing by the police. We let her down.

DCI Harvey interrupted. "Listen, it's not good that as a force we didn't follow up the MisPer. But so many kids go missing these days. We can't follow up on every one; we don't have the resources. We can't track them all." She nodded, as if to reassure Scott.

Raj continued, "The unit got a call from her two days ago, saying she wanted to come back – she sounded panicky, said someone was after her. Then she hung up."

"Did she mention Johnny to them?" Scott asked.

"No, guv, but they said she sounded scared."

Scott nodded and rubbed his chin. "Johnny could be lying. Or if he's telling the truth, he got her addicted to drugs to control her. In time he could do the same to Jenna. Abby and I will visit the residential unit tomorrow. Sian, check with other residential units, see if other girls have gone missing."

"No probs," Sian said.

Scott addressed DCI Harvey. "Ma'am, can we get a protection order in place for tomorrow and get Jenna out? We need to get her back to Benedict's."

The DCI casually nodded her approval.

"Thank you, ma'am. Sian, you and Mike can go and get Jenna?

"Raj." Scott smiled. "CCTV duties for you, fella."

Raj groaned as he was delegated to watching hours and hours of footage.

"Check footage around the train station and the Unicorn. See if you can spot any sightings of Libby."

Raj gave the weakest of nods.

Before breaking up the meeting, Scott paused and reflected on something Raj had highlighted.

"Actually, doughnut boy, can you find out more about this youth club as soon as you can?"

This was met with a wide smile and an enthusiastic nod.

Scott ended with, "Right, team, go grab some shut-eye. Lots to do tomorrow."

12

Benedict's residential unit was on the outskirts of Hove, tucked away at the end of a cul-de-sac away from prying eyes. Passers-by and residents would be oblivious to the vulnerable, exploited and abandoned children living amongst them.

The council-run unit housed fourteen children between the ages of ten and seventeen. It was a safe haven, a place to stay if they needed protection, or somewhere to escape the difficult circumstances in their young lives.

Some of the children had been neglected by parents who faced their own battles with drugs, alcohol, gambling or abusive relationships. Others had suffered physical or sexual abuse at the hands of people they trusted.

As safe havens went, the appearance of Benedict's didn't offer the warmest of welcomes. Three two-storey, featureless square buildings with flat roofs formed the main complex. The sandstone-coloured brick walls and large, obtrusive, military-like spotlights positioned close to the roofline made the place feel less than welcoming. A six-foot-high, closeboard fence and an imposing, dense treeline surrounded the perimeter. Dating back to the early 1970s, residential units were often seen as an indictment of an uncaring society. Very little thought went into their design and purpose. The design only added to the perception of it being a detention centre rather than a place of safety and compassion.

Scott and Abby pulled into the compound and parked in the solitary parking bay for visitors – another sign that few outsiders visited. As they walked towards the entrance, both officers surveyed the characterless establishment that greeted them. A hanging flower basket with wilting blue lobelia that were in dire need of water helped to soften the entrance, but not much.

A quick look between them confirmed they were both thinking the same thing. If it was this grim outside, what was it like inside?

Despite flashing their warrant cards at the CCTV camera positioned above the door, it was a while before someone unlocked the door for them. Their every move was being monitored by the camera, which had likely locked on to them the moment they drove through the gated entrance.

Scott and Abby stepped into the entrance hall, little more than a sparse corridor. The walls were painted magnolia. The well-trodden, scratched, functional wooden floors and ceiling strip lights reinforced the basic and practical purpose of the unit.

A few tatty poster boards scattered at odd intervals broke up the bland walls. Each board displayed posters and notices of various activities and clubs. In the corner of one was the obligatory rules and regulations about behaviour, health and safety, added almost as an afterthought.

A lady wearing a floral dress and dark grey jacket approached them. Her outfit reminded Scott of the images that used to adorn the Laura Ashley clothing catalogues. So nineties. Her long bob of light brown hair and unflattering fringe only enhanced her outdated appearance.

She greeted them with a warm smile. "Hello there, I'm Jean Temple, the unit manager. How can I help you?" Her voice was clear, crisp and precise. It was likely honed from years of dealing with and supporting difficult children and the various support agencies.

Scott held up a picture. "Jenna Wade, is she one of yours? We found her at a property with an eighteen-year-old male she claims is her boyfriend. She says she's sixteen?"

Jean immediately recognised her. "She is indeed. Fifteen going on thirty and growing up too quickly. She's gone walkabouts again. They do it all the time."

Scott and Abby exchanged glances at the woman's casual attitude.

"How long has she been missing?" Abby asked.

"Three days now."

"Did you report her?"

She gave Abby an accusatory look and a curt reply. "Yes, we do that immediately. Often they come back after a couple of days on their own."

For all the security, Scott was concerned that actual monitoring of the residents was lacking here.

"Did you hear about Libby Stevens?"

Jean nodded, her only reaction to Scott's enquiry. "Yes, we were informed about that yesterday. Such sad news."

Scott examined her face as he questioned her authenticity.

Is she really bothered? How many years has she been doing this? No doubt she's seen many kids in her care come and go. She probably couldn't give a flying toss these days and is holding out for her pension.

Scott continued, "Does Jenna have many friends here?"

A shake of the woman's head was the only response given.

Her terse replies were beginning to grate on Scott. Anyone would think she was being formally interviewed.

He waited in silence, hoping the lull would force her to continue.

It did. "She pretty much keeps herself to herself. Jenna didn't really know her mum and dad... been in care since she was a baby. Jenna can be pretty tricky and has run away from all the foster places she's been sent to. But I can't blame her, to be honest."

Scott glanced around. *I can't blame her either if this is all she has to look forward to.*

He asked, "Do you know much about her boyfriend, Johnny Wright?"

"I'm afraid not. I heard his name being mentioned occasionally when I stumbled upon conversations between them on the phone, but nothing more, Inspector."

Abby folded her arms. "You said earlier that kids go walkabout all the time. Any more missing children from here?"

Jean stared at Abby. "No. I think we've had our fair share, don't you? Besides, you hear about runaways all the time, and not just from residential units like ours. They're fodder to those preying on the vulnerable, and kids like Jenna are two a penny."

"Thank you, Jean, you've been helpful," Scott said. "Jenna's being picked up under a police protection order this morning, as we're concerned for her safety and welfare. Two of my officers will be returning her to this unit."

"I'll look forward to it." He detected a hint of sarcasm in her voice.

Scott and Abby left.

Abby sighed as she got back in the car. "That was hard work. Talk about cooperation between agencies."

"She's certainly no Mary Poppins," Scott said with a grimace.

13

Scott threw his jacket over the back of his chair before going in search of Raj. It was never hard to identify Raj's desk – organised chaos best described his workstation. How Raj managed his files was a mystery. But whenever pressed and without hesitation, he was able to identify and retrieve the information in question, much to Scott's surprise.

Raj was busy at work when Scott arrived. Scott grabbed a Bourbon biscuit from a half-empty packet on the corner of Raj's desk. Biting into it, he grimaced at its softness and was tempted to spit it out.

He swallowed and looked over his shoulder to see Sian and Mike returning.

"Package dropped off?" he asked Mike.

Mike nodded to confirm as he headed to the water cooler.

Scott turned his attention back to Raj, who was busily tidying his notes in his DI's presence. "How did you get on with the CCTV trawl, Raj?"

"Got some good stuff, guv. The CCTV footage shows Johnny Wright arguing with Libby Stevens outside the

Unicorn pub the night before she was found dead." Raj added with a raised brow, "Jenna was present too."

"Time?" Scott perched on the edge of the desk, his hands in his pockets.

"Nine twenty-five p.m."

Scott fumed. Johnny had lied. "So much for not stopping or talking, you lying git."

Raj continued, "She looked disturbed, guv. She was pacing around, waving her arms frantically. It looked like she was screaming at Johnny. Jenna was trying to step in the middle of them. Johnny and Jenna eventually walk off, but Libby heads into the Unicorn."

"Think I need another chat with Johnny, don't you?"

Raj nodded in agreement as he chewed the top of his pen and leant back in his chair. He looked pleased with the results of his hard work.

"There's more, guv. Libby left the Unicorn pub with the landlord. They headed around the back. The landlord returned about ten minutes later. Libby appeared fifteen minutes after him. She seemed a little disorientated in the footage and stumbled a little before dropping out of the camera's view."

Scott rubbed his chin, deep in thought. The latest insight into Libby's final few hours troubled him. Disappearing with the landlord suggested one thing.

"We need to get the landlord in, too."

Scott turned to locate Mike and shouted across the desks, "Don't get too comfortable, Mike. Go pick up the landlord of the Unicorn. We need him to help us with our enquiries into Libby's last known movements."

Mike lifted his large frame from the creaking chair. "I'll check to see if he's got CCTV for his pub?"

"Yep, good call, Mike."

Scott walked up behind Abby, who was seated at her

desk. He tapped her on the shoulder. "Fancy grabbing an early lunch? We'll be busy this afternoon when the landlord comes in."

"You don't need to ask me twice!" responded Abby.

She grabbed her purse and followed as they wound their way through the corridors and stairs of the station. The weather was shaping up nicely outside, the warm early sunshine hitting their faces as they emerged from beneath the station entrance canopy.

"Where are we off to?" Abby asked.

"How about Munch, down the road?" suggested Scott.

"Perfect, I'll have my usual."

"Spanish omelette and chips?"

"What else? You know me, creature of habit."

14

Munch coffee shop was a small café situated a few minutes' walk from the station. It was a popular stopping-off point for many officers who wanted to grab a quick sandwich or hot meal.

From the outside, it could have been mistaken for an internet café, with its row of white contemporary plastic dining chairs positioned along the front window. The café was clean and modern-looking inside, with white walls edged with green painted borders. An aroma of freshly brewed coffee hung in the air, together with various aromas of hot food that wafted occasionally from the kitchen.

After ordering, Scott and Abby grabbed a table near the far left wall.

Staring into his coffee, the trail of steam wafting up, the smell of freshly percolated coffee stirring his senses, Scott felt lost. Over the past few years, he had tried hard to cover the cracks in his soul and the pain that seeped from them daily.

Whilst sipping on her latte, Abby looked up at Scott. "Guv, off the record, is something bothering you? You've been preoccupied since yesterday."

"It's just been hard the last few days, Abby. Seeing Libby and her short life destroyed like that hit me hard. I went to see Becky and Tina." He mumbled, "That just wiped me out."

"Yes, I can imagine." She studied Scott for a brief moment. "I look at Sophie, and I know I'd be lost without her. Yes, she can be a pain in the arse, and she's always glued to her phone. Getting a conversation out of her is like getting blood out of a stone. She's still my flesh and blood though... she's still my little girl." Abby leant in and lowered her voice. "Listen, guv, it's important not to bottle it up. I don't know if I can be of any help, but when things get to you, you can always give me a shout. Sometimes it helps to talk about it."

Scott knew Abby was trying to offer support in her own unique way. She was a good officer and a good friend too, someone he trusted implicitly, both personally and professionally. But he wasn't about to make a scene and start blubbing, even though he could feel the emotion rising from the pit of his stomach. His vision blurred, and the swirling mass threatened to engulf him again.

He took a deep breath. "I appreciate it, Abby. I know all the officers are finding this case hard, but as a parent, it makes me angry that shit like this still goes on."

They paused when the waitress arrived with their food, then thanked her as she left.

Abby sighed. "Yes, it's shit. It's bad enough when you've got the exploitation of women, but when it's kids, it makes me sick."

"Yup," was Scott's only answer as he tucked into his hot New Yorker melt.

Abby changed the subject. "What do you make of Johnny, then?"

"He's a slippery bugger. I get a strange feeling he seems to enjoy the power trip he gets from pulling younger girls." He paused to wipe his mouth before taking a sip of his coffee.

"He has to be connected to Libby's death. He's seen on CCTV footage having an argument with her the night before. He now has another girlfriend in tow, and there are too many similarities. The gifts, their similar ages, and those identical tattoos." Scott shrugged. "Anyone would think he's branding them."

"He's not being entirely truthful with us, is he?"

"No. We need to bring him in for further questioning this afternoon. You can come in with me on the interview with the landlord. Get Raj to pick up Johnny for us. That way when we've spoken to the landlord and Johnny this afternoon, we'll have a clearer picture concerning the last few hours of Libby's life."

15

The warm June afternoon sunshine greeted Scott and Abby. With a full afternoon of interviews to get through, they trudged back to the station, both relaxed and tired from devouring their lunches.

A strong, pungent smell hit Scott as they strode in, the origin of which seemed to trail back to Mike's desk. Both of them glared at Mike.

"What?" he shouted.

The DS had a small napkin tucked into the top of his collar, to stop the splashes from his chicken dhansak curry peppering the front of his white shirt. Mike shrugged in defiance when Abby reminded him that he wasn't at home and went on to say that they would all smell of curry by the time he was finished.

"A man's got to eat. You're just jealous," was all he said. He dipped his naan bread into the dhansak sauce.

Scott escaped to the sanctuary of his office and pushed open a window. The smell of sea air was far more inviting and neutralised the curry smell. He fired up his computer and printed off the information he needed, then logged off.

He gazed at the small double photo frame that sat discreetly beside his monitor, and time stood still. One was a photo of him and Tina taken on their honeymoon. A selfie of them lying in a hammock one evening, giggling. He smiled as he remembered how they'd attempted to pose gracefully for the photo whilst hanging on for dear life.

The other was a picture of all three of them taken on the beach. He studied Becky's innocent smile and face, her cheeks tinged red in the sun. She was sitting on the pebble beach, a fast-melting ice cream in her hand that dripped off her elbow.

Innocent fun.

Happier times. Happier memories.

THE LANDLORD of the Unicorn pub shifted nervously in his seat in the interview room, an observation not missed by Scott as he and Abby entered. Mark Renshaw was a large-framed man of average height who appeared to enjoy drinking his profits, judging by the shirt buttons straining to hold in his large beer belly. Renshaw, sitting alone, had waived his right to representation.

Abby cautioned him and explained that he had been brought in to help them with their enquiries into the death of Libby Stevens. His shocked acknowledgement was accompanied by more jittery movements in the chair.

Scott rested both elbows on the desk, his hands interlocked. He locked his gaze on Renshaw as Abby nudged a picture of Libby towards him.

"Have you seen this girl before?" Abby asked.

It was a moment or two before the man looked down at the smiling picture of Libby. He stared at her photo, his eyelids flickering, his jaw muscles tightening. Scott knew the next thing that would come out of Renshaw's mouth would be a lie.

"Can't say I recognise her, to be honest," he said.

Scott exchanged a brief glance with Abby before she pushed forward a second picture of Libby. In that one, her cold, pallid, lifeless features were staring up from the mortuary table.

Renshaw cleared his throat and shifted with more unease. His hand trembled as he held a cup of water to his mouth.

A tactic to buy some time to think.

The landlord shook his head once. "No, still don't recognise her."

Abby pushed her trump card towards Renshaw. It was a still image of him leaving the pub with Libby. The image froze him to the spot, the large gulp giving away his guilt.

"Now, Mr Renshaw, shall we start again?" Scott said forcefully. He'd had enough of this prat wasting his time. "She was fifteen," he said slowly and deliberately.

In a low murmur, Renshaw replied, "How was I supposed to know? I didn't ask her age."

"How much did you pay her?" Abby asked.

There was a lengthy pause before Renshaw sighed in defeat. "Look, I know her. She hangs around the pub, looking for tricks. She came looking for drugs. I just helped her out."

"In return for what?"

"She was desperate," he replied defensively.

"She must have been," said Abby with a raised brow.

"Libby had no money; she wanted one last hit. She was pretty wired, scared almost. We went down the alley, did the deed; I gave her the gear and left. I swear that's all."

"How much did she want?" asked Scott.

"She wanted fifty pounds for a blow job."

"But you wouldn't give her that much?"

He nodded wearily. "I said I wanted a shag for that much."

"What did you bargain it down to? What is the going rate for sex with an underage girl who's desperate for drugs and is now dead just hours after you saw her?"

A long silence followed Scott's question. The quagmire Renshaw found himself in threatened to swallow him up.

"Sorry, I can't hear you," Scott shouted, his patience wearing thin.

"Twenty quid," he finally admitted. "But I swear I had nothing to do with her death. I was in the pub until closing time and then cleaned up for a couple of hours. It was gone one a.m. by the time I went to bed!"

Scott and Abby exchanged a look of disgust.

"Twenty pounds' worth of smack." Scott glowered. "Can anyone account for your movements for the rest of the night?"

"No. I live alone."

Scott paused for a moment before continuing, "Your bruises have healed well."

Renshaw stared at Scott for a moment, caught off guard by the change in direction of the questioning.

"What do you mean?"

"The aggravated assault on you two months ago... The pub all sorted now?"

"Err... yes," he grumbled under his breath. Renshaw looked down, unwilling to look either officer in the eye.

"Well, don't worry, we haven't closed the file yet. Our enquiries are still ongoing. I'm sure we'll find those responsible and why they targeted you," Scott said in a harsher tone. His eyes bored into the top of Renshaw's head.

"We'll need you to provide a DNA swab and fingerprint swipe to eliminate you from our enquiries, Mr Renshaw," Abby added.

A dejected Renshaw gave her request a solitary nod. His shoulders had dropped; his breathing came in short, rapid bursts.

Abby said, "For the tape, Mr Renshaw has nodded his head."

She concluded the interview by advising Renshaw, "We'll be applying to the CPS to charge you with coercion and having sex with a minor."

Renshaw buried his face in his hands.

16

Time was fast escaping him today. Scott was desperate to get the team together for a debrief before the end of the shift. He agreed with Abby that she would visit Jenna again for another chat, and Scott would interview Johnny, who was waiting in an adjoining interview room.

As he made his way there, Scott's phone buzzed. It was a message from Cara.

Hope all is well with you. You free tomorrow evening? X

Scott smiled, quickly tapping out his reply.

Yep, 7.30 p.m., but might have to let you down at the last minute, as have a lot on.

He dropped his phone back in his pocket as it buzzed again. He'd look at her reply later.

It was gone seven p.m. and the time the team had already reconvened in the briefing room. Scott had been delayed by the arrival of an urgent job. A report had flashed up on his screen, sent from the duty inspector regarding a reported missing person. Any MisPer report was always actioned immediately.

Scott scanned the details and found that the usual information threw up nothing of substance.

Christine Newland, 43, married mum of one daughter. Long brown wavy hair, lives in Tongdean Avenue, Hove.

Left for work yesterday morning. Employers confirmed to husband that Christine left work in a hurry following a phone call at 12.30 p.m., but husband says she never came home.

Last seen leaving place of work in North Street. Behaviour is out of character for her. She is always home before her daughter returns from school.

Drives a red Renault Clio FZ 05 GHT, which is missing.

She is not answering her mobile phone.

Reported missing by Alan Newland, husband.

Scott tasked Sian to follow up on the report as soon as the debrief was over. He instructed her to do a risk assessment, in particular, to look at the usual things like self-harm, abduction, vulnerability, physical and mental health issues, previous disappearances, etc. The husband needed calling too in case she'd returned. If not, then she was to go round there.

Scott had left her with a final instruction. "If in doubt, think the worst until the contrary is proved."

Despite Sian being new to the team, she'd proved more than capable of using her own intuition. For that reason, Scott enjoyed the chance to push her, as he did with most members of his team. The one exception was Raj, who Scott felt was a rough diamond who still needed closer supervision.

As Scott made his way to the briefing room, he reflected on the team's current caseload. If they weren't busy enough already, to have a MisPer now meant the likelihood of having to split his resources. Or worse still, he would have to ask the DCI for extra resources from other teams.

17

An assortment of aromas assaulted Scott's nostrils the minute he entered the briefing room. Smells that set off an embarrassing rumble from deep within his stomach. Raj had taken care of everyone's dietary needs by ordering two large Domino's pizzas, a Hawaiian and a meat feast, plus garlic dough bites, which the team gratefully helped themselves to.

Scott grabbed a slice of pizza and stood by the whiteboard, slice flopping in his hand.

"Right, gang, I'm tired, as I'm sure most of you are, so let's get on with this and get home. Sian, what can you tell us about any other missing girls?"

Wiping her mouth with a paper napkin, Sian said, "Social services only came back to me at six this evening. We have Jasmine Reed, aged fifteen from Brighton. She was in care but went missing from Tindale residential unit four months ago. She was fished out of the water near Sherborne Wharf in Birmingham. She was beaten to death and had evidence of an overdose, according to toxicology reports.

"Then we have Rishi Mehta, again aged fifteen. An Asian

girl missing from Manchester, believed to be in the Sussex area recently. I spoke to Greythorne High School in Manchester. She was last seen at the school gates five months ago and had been in foster care at the time. The school said that Rishi had been sent home for repeatedly texting in class. Apparently, she was texting her boyfriend, but they couldn't give me a name. There was evidence on her Facebook page that she was chatting to a guy from Brighton, but the account was fake and has not been used since."

"IP address?" Scott asked.

"Still looking at that, guv."

DCI Harvey slipped in the door whilst Sian was speaking and eased into a seat at the top end of the table.

Scott said, "Both girls were fifteen. Unconnected murders? Possible, but three girls aged fifteen missing on our patch or killed? That worries me."

"Guv, Jasmine also had a heart-shaped tattoo on her ankle with a love inscription in it," Sian added.

"What the hell," blurted out Scott. "Sorry, ma'am."

The DCI waved her hand, nonplussed.

"Could the girls be linked to Johnny?" Mike suggested.

Scott nodded thoughtfully. "The tattoos are telling evidence and more than a coincidence. I reinterviewed Johnny this afternoon but got little more out of him. Shame we didn't have the social services information earlier today. I put it to him that after the row, he went back to track down Libby and got Jenna to cover for him. But he wasn't budging from his story, so I need to put some more pressure on him. Abby?"

"I went to see Jenna again this afternoon. I tried to get through to her, but she kept repeating that Libby was jealous. She reckons Libby took offence because they were together, nothing else. Despite telling her how Johnny plied Libby with booze, drugs and showered her with gifts just like he's doing with her, she's convinced we've got it all wrong. Jenna did let go a bit. She said Libby was saying all this mad stuff but was sure it was Libby's attempt to break them up."

"What type of stuff?" Scott asked.

"That Johnny had got her into drink and drugs. He'd made her sleep with other men, lots of men, said that Jenna was next. And that they'd used Libby and moved her from place to place. That Libby had looked down and confused, but said she was going to put a stop to it. Jenna was adamant Johnny would never do that to her. 'Johnny loves me,' she kept saying defiantly."

"She's been brainwashed, guv," offered Raj.

"It's not uncommon," added DCI Harvey. "Vulnerable kids see some of these men as their saviours, their ticket to a better life. It's often the first time anyone has shown them love and affection. They fall for it hook, line and sinker. And because of that, will say anything to protect them. It's unlikely she'll testify against him."

Scott paced slowly around the room. "Well, it's possible he grooms them, uses them and moves on to the next girl. Just abandons them when they are of no use to him... But by then, they're even more dependent and vulnerable. We must be missing something."

"Like what?" asked Sian.

"Libby was your average fifteen-year-old schoolgirl, and then within a year, she's a drugged-up kid, looking for sex to satisfy her cravings. That transformation happened for a reason, and that reason points to Johnny."

Raj interjected, "Why did she do a runner? What happened that freaked her out?"

His questions were met with silence from those around the table.

Scott shook his head, the lack of clarity taxing his brain. "Johnny's grooming the girls, breaking them down, and making them so dependent on him that they'll do anything for him, including sleeping with other guys. The girls are vulnerable, their self-esteem gets lower and lower, and their addiction gets stronger and stronger. And when he's done with them for whatever reason, he moves them along or dumps them onto the streets to fend for themselves."

Abby added, "Where they inevitably end up working the streets. That would explain the girls in Manchester and Birmingham, and when Libby threatened to blow the lid, she may have paid for it with her life."

Scott frowned. "The question is who did it? I'm not sure about the landlord of the Unicorn; he's too pathetic to kill someone. We need to focus our investigation on Johnny."

Raj spoke. "Guv, I've seen footage of Johnny talking with another white male. I can't get a good description, but I can pull off stills first thing."

Scott approved with a nod. "This could be the tip of the iceberg. Johnny and others unknown could be moving girls around the country. Something like this is organised. There must be gangs in other cities taking them. We could be looking at a national network of trafficking underage girls. Johnny is just one small link; he's clever, but not that clever... not enough to run this. He's just a scrote doing the dirty work for someone else. We also have to consider that these are just the girls we know about. There are kids who disappear, go missing or run off every year who are never reported missing."

He paused to take a bite of the meat feast slice that was drooping from a napkin in his hand. Even though he wasn't feeling hungry, pizza had an uncanny knack of making his stomach think it was. Each bite soothed the aching emptiness he felt inside.

Scott's thoughts were interrupted by DCI Harvey's phone ringing.

The team paused for a moment while the DCI listened, nodded. She replied, "Thanks for letting me know. We'll be over right away."

She gave a long hard sigh as she hung up. "I think your job just got a little harder, DI Baker. A member of the public has just reported finding the body of a middle-aged female. Found on the edge of Hove Park near the junction of Woodland Drive and Chartfield."

18

Hove Park was located to the north of Hove, a popular park with residents, dog walkers and runners. It featured a mix of large open grass, mature trees, flowerbeds and recreational facilities. Its boundary was lined with tall, mature elm trees that gave a picturesque look to the area.

The last remnants of daylight were diminishing fast by the time Scott and Abby arrived on the scene. The scenes-of-crime officers were busy. A white forensic tent had been erected where the victim had been found; arc lights illuminated the scene. The officers were working quickly to secure the area by marking it out and beginning the early forensic examination before day turned to night.

Scott and Abby signed into the scene log that PC Oju was maintaining at the cordon of the scene. The police activity had attracted its usual flock of curious passers-by and residents.

Scott and Abby spent a few moments putting on forensic suits before venturing into a small, dense, overgrown wooded area that skirted the southern edge of the park.

As he stood there, Scott looked around to develop a mental picture of the crime scene and its surrounding landscape. From the road, it was unlikely that anyone would have seen any activity taking place in the middle of this area.

He carefully pushed the branches to one side as he approached the scene, his legs soon disappearing up to his knees in overgrown foliage. Abby followed a few steps behind him, cursing the fact that she'd worn her court shoes.

Not the most ideal footwear when traipsing around the woodland floor.

The cracking of twigs and the crunching of leaves beneath their feet alerted Matt Allan, the crime scene manager, to their arrival. He was kneeling in the undergrowth, organising evidence bags that had already been gathered.

The blue tent glowed brightly due to the illumination of the arc lights that had been set up inside. Through the material, ghoulish shadows danced around as SOCOs examined the body. Intermittent flashes of new light permeated the tent walls as the whole scene was documented and photographed.

Scott took a moment to look around. It was hard to evaluate the crime scene effectively, given his view was obscured in every direction. A thick impenetrable wall of trees, shrubs and bushes closed in from all sides, and impending darkness limited his view. He looked up at the last few glimmers of daylight attempting to worm their way through the gaps in the upper canopy of the trees.

Before long, the surrounding area would take on a different identity. It would go from a playground for kids and a safe recreational area for pensioners to walk their dogs, to a black sea of darkness that few would brave crossing at night. It would become a landscape for nocturnal wildlife to play and hunt.

SOCO Matt Allan looked up. "Scott, how you doing, buddy?"

"Evening, Matt. We were just about to knock off for the evening when we got this call."

"No rest for the wicked, eh?"

Scott exhaled loudly. "Go on then, what have you got so far?"

"We've got a woman, probably in her forties, found in a shallow grave of earth and leaves. A dog walker stumbled upon the find when he went to retrieve his dog that had wandered into here. He found the dog scraping away the debris. When he pulled the animal away, a hand poked through. The poor bloke practically shit himself."

Scott and Abby pulled back the flap of the tent and peered in, keen not to disturb or contaminate the scene before the forensic team had completed their sweep. From Scott's position, he could see the outline of a woman lying on her side. The debris had been moved to reveal one arm contorted back on itself, the palm facing up, her face bloodied and dirty, her white blouse unbuttoned and stained dark. One shoe was missing, no doubt due to a struggle or being dragged through the undergrowth. Her hair looked dishevelled and matted to one side of her face.

Scott made a mental note to request the cordon be immediately extended around the perimeter of the park. At first light, a sweep could be done by uniformed officers to locate her other shoe and any other items that could be connected to her.

Matt carried on with his initial assessment. "She seems to have heavy head wounds and..." He paused, looking at the pair of them. "She's had her nipples cut off." He shrugged. "Weird, if you ask me."

"Anything else?" Scott asked.

"We found a handbag found beside the body. Purse and

phone are still inside, so not sure robbery is the motive, more likely sexual. Her driving licence IDs her as Christine Newland. She lives close by in Tongdean Avenue. She has a pendant necklace on with the initial C, so it could belong to her."

Scott frowned. His missing person. "Fuck's sake."

"What?" Matt asked.

"She's a MisPer that came in this afternoon. I gave it to Sian to follow up," he said, massaging his forehead.

"Want me to inform the husband, guv?" Abby asked.

"No, it's fine. I'll break the news. Get on to the station and put in a request for a FLO to meet me there in fifteen minutes. You need to head off. It will be a late one. Your kids need you home... Go on."

"You sure?"

"Go," he barked, "before I change my mind and get you to do door to door. Uniform can do the witness door to door for a few houses close by and the nosey parkers by the roadside. We can follow up tomorrow morning if there's anything of interest. Mike and Sian are on at six a.m. They can deal with it then."

"Thanks, I need to go via my in-laws to grab Adam and Sophie before facing a mountain of ironing, housework and preparing Adam's packed lunch for the following day."

Scott couldn't help but laugh and shake his head in dismay as he watched Abby trample through the wooded area, swearing to herself as the protective suit snagged on thorns.

"Is the path on the way here?" Scott asked.

"Yep, she's been informed. She's due shortly. You wanna speak to her?"

"I'll catch up with her later. Off to break the news now and confirm if this is the MisPer." He pursed his lips in frustration.

Matt held up a small clear evidence bag with a picture in it. "Take this. It was in her handbag."

Scott held it up in the near darkness. He shone a light from his phone screen and saw the picture of a couple sitting at a table across from each other. A sparkling turquoise sea offered an idyllic backdrop as they shared a glass of wine. No doubt a tropical holiday somewhere.

He looked back at Matt and raised an eyebrow.

"Good luck, mate."

19

PC Andrea Smith, the family liaison officer, was already parked outside the address in Tongdean Avenue by the time Scott arrived. The road was an affluent mix of large, detached properties with deep-fronted driveways, some of which swept away behind electrically operated security gates. Tall hedges offered further privacy. Any prospective buyers would find it hard to get change from one and a half million pounds if they went shopping down this street.

The house Scott was interested in was an impressive family home. Matching front and garage doors added to the expensive feel of the property, and well-proportioned bay-fronted windows offered a tantalising glimpse inside. A van was parked in front of the garage doors.

Scott glanced at the van's signage: Newland Electrical Contractors, All commercial and domestic electrical work undertaken.

Looking up, he could see that the house had been extended into the roof space, adding a further floor.

The electrical business must be booming.

After pressing the doorbell next to the large, double light oak doors, he and Andrea waited. The glass panel insets provided a clear view into a wide hallway with a shiny ivory-coloured tiled floor and a wide staircase towards the rear, leading up to the first floor.

An eager, stocky middle-aged man came into view and opened the door. Scott assumed this to be Christine's husband. His eyes were bloodshot and small, his breath hurried.

His worried gaze shifted between the two strangers on his doorstep before he shot further glances past them, as if he expected to find his wife.

Given the man's creased pink shirt and unkempt wavy black hair, Scott assumed that Mr Newland had had very little sleep. He was joined a few seconds later by a girl no older than fourteen or fifteen. She stood there in a black vest top and jeans, one hand nervously fiddling with a black hair-band that was wrapped around her other wrist.

Scott and Andrea presented their warrant cards. "I'm Detective Inspector Baker, and this is Police Constable Andrea Smith. Are you Mr Newland?"

The man nodded. "Yes, I'm Alan Newland, and this is our daughter, Lucy," he said, shooting a quick glance at his daughter, who stared into space. "Is this about my wife? Have you found her?"

"It is. May we come in?"

Alan Newland showed them into a large formal living room with two large, brown leather sofas facing each other and an expensive-looking glass rectangular table in between them. A flat-screen TV hung above the fireplace. In one corner of the room, Scott clocked a large bookcase with hundreds of books. Tall ornate vases covered in a mosaic of small, squared mirror pieces sat either side of each sofa, adding to the opulent feel.

Mr Newland motioned for them to sit down.

Before Scott took his seat, he turned to Alan Newland. "Is it possible to talk to you in private for a moment?"

Alan hesitantly looked towards his daughter.

In a faint voice he said, "Lucy, darling, can you go to your bedroom just for a few moments?"

With an anxious look and fear burning in her eyes, she turned to leave. Before she did, she glanced back nervously with narrowed eyes and tight lips.

Scott sat and looked at Alan Newland. He saw a man who was beside himself with worry. Restless hours of wondering where his wife was had robbed him of any energy. Now Scott was about to destroy his life.

"There isn't an easy way to tell you this, Mr Newland, but we've just found a body. It's a woman in her mid-forties with long brown wavy hair. We can't be certain as yet to her identity. However, we've found evidence at the scene that links her to this address."

Scott's words seemed to have no effect on Mr Newland. The man was likely in a state of shock and unable to comprehend what he'd just been told. In their line of work, difficult news like this was often met with a variety of reactions.

Scott continued, "The body was found not far from here. A handbag was close by, and inside it were a mobile phone and purse. There was a driving licence in the name of Christine Newland with this address. And we also found a picture." Scott held it up for Mr Newland. "Is this your wife?"

Newland nodded, then placed his hands over his face. He lurched forward, his shaking shoulders the only clue to his silent cries. PC Smith joined him. She placed one hand on his back and gave him a sympathetic pat.

"What happened to her?" Newland asked, looking at Scott, his eyes heavy with tears that escaped down his cheeks.

"We're not entirely sure. The forensic team is still on-site, but early indications suggest the victim suffered a serious assault." Scott chose not to cause the man any further pain by suggesting a sexual nature to the assault. "Did your wife have a necklace when she disappeared?"

"Yes," he replied and ran a hand through his wavy, unkempt hair. "It was a thin silver curb chain with a swirly C pendant."

Scott was certain now that this was indeed his wife.

"I know it's a difficult time for you, but we'll need you to identify if it's your wife. Andrea is a family liaison officer and will remain here to help in any way she can. Tomorrow, she will take you to the mortuary after the post-mortem has been completed."

Alan Newland tried to compose himself. His eyes were restless, his mind clearly trying to comprehend the enormity of the news he'd just received. "No, I can't wait that long. I need to see her. I need to see her immediately." He elicited a groan from deep within his chest, his breath jerky and heavy. "What am I going to tell Lucy?"

Scott didn't have an answer; how could he? He felt the man's pain. Alan Newland had just lost his wife, a person he'd committed to spending the rest of his life with. His wife and the mother of their child.

Nevertheless, Scott had a murder to investigate. In cases involving suspicious deaths, close family were always the first suspects of the investigating team. Sympathy would come later. Now, Scott needed to remain objective.

"Mr Newland, the next few hours are vital. I know it's difficult, but we'll need to speak to you in the morning. Andrea Smith can take you to see the body this evening and then bring you to the station tomorrow."

In between the sobs, Alan Newland looked up and nodded meekly.

20

Witnessing a post-mortem examination in the morning wasn't something Scott wished to ever do. Although his visit would be far less traumatic than Alan Newland's visit the night before. The man had confirmed his wife's identity late in what Andrea had called a painful and very sad appointment.

By the time he arrived, Abby and Cara were deeply engrossed in conversation in the office. They were sipping large mugs of tea and working their way through a packet of chocolate digestive biscuits.

The conversation stopped dead in its tracks the minute he walked into the room. Both looked at him like startled children who'd been caught raiding the contents of the tuck shop. Their eyes were fixed wide, half-eaten biscuits in one hand, a mug of tea in the other.

He wondered if they had been talking about him.

"Should my ears be burning?" he asked, glancing between them with suspicion in his eyes.

Abby let out a cackle of laughter. "Erm, no... but if you're into period pains, then pull up a chair!" Cara choked on her tea as she fought against her own laugh.

Feeling suitably embarrassed, Scott retraced his steps, walking backwards out of the room. "I'll leave you two experts to discuss that topic in peace... but another time. We've got work to do."

"Party pooper," Cara shouted after him.

Scott could never really put his finger on why the mortuary smelt the way it did. Cara was adamant it didn't smell at all. No doubt her sense of smell had become accustomed to the heady mix of detergents, sanitisers and decomposing flesh.

Most people would never need to step into a mortuary unless it was their final resting place, or family was coming to identify a body. Every mortuary Scott had been to bore striking similarities. The solemn surroundings seemed to drain the colour out of the environment as much as it did from the cadavers – everything was a grey or off-white. The magnolia-speckled lino floors wrapped halfway up the walls. The coldness of the metal tables, metal benches and fridge units added to the emptiness. This truly was a grim place to work.

For Cara and the mortuary technicians, it was their office. They appeared oblivious to the cloying smell that hung in the air and crawled into every fibre of clothing. It was normal for them to see bodies neatly packed in fridges awaiting collection by the sombre undertakers coming to collect their clients. Yet the technicians laughed and joked as they would in any office. They talked about their daily lives, the irritating habits of their partners, what they were cooking for dinner later. They even discussed the fractured and hazy recollections of their night on the town.

The cadaver Scott had come to see was on the first of three tables in the examination room, in the middle of the room. To the right was the bank of fridge doors, and to the left was a long, stainless steel work surface with sinks and water hoses. Other than the gentle hum of the air conditioning, the room was silent.

Surprisingly, for her trade, Cara had very few tools to work with. A silver tray to her side had been laid out with two scalpels of different lengths, a black rubber mallet, a screwdriver, two soup ladles, a pair of scissors, and a steel implement in the shape of a T that had a sharp flat tip on the long edge. Scott and Abby stood on one side of the cadaver whilst Cara stood on the other.

She began her procedure.

In the light of day, Scott could see the victim clearly for the first time. She was a well-proportioned woman with chubby cheeks that had no doubt once sported a warm smile. Her long brown hair on her left side was matted with a thick, dried, black crust of earth and blood.

Cara carried out her preliminary visual inspection of the cadaver, capturing her notes in a handheld voice recorder. Scott and Abby said nothing while the pathologist gave a running commentary of any visible marks like pinpricks, tattoos, birthmarks or moles. She moved on to an overall summary of the condition of the body, focusing on any external signs that could have contributed to her cause of death.

A mortuary technician whom Cara called Neil wheeled over the handheld rotary saw on its trolley. He was a slim-bodied man, with thick-framed glasses and long messy hair that was greying. Neil fired up the saw to make sure it was working, its high-powered motor spinning into action, making a whining noise similar to a dentist's drill.

Cara gave Neil a nod as she took the instrument from him. She began by making an incision behind one ear of the cadaver. She traced her scalpel around the back of the head to the other ear. She then carefully peeled back her scalp over the top of the head to partially cover her face, creating a ghoulish mask more fitting at Halloween.

Cara then switched on the rotary saw and began to carve around the top of the dead woman's skull. Scott flinched when the saw cut into the coarse material of the skull.

Abby had a similar reaction. From behind her face mask, her eyes narrowed as small bone fragments flew in all directions. Finally using the T-shaped turnkey, Cara prised away the cut section of the skull to reveal a light-pink shiny brain that was starting to turn creamy brown in places.

Scott remained silent; Cara, meanwhile, was delicately pulling the brain out of the skull to expose the optic nerves. Using a long slender scalpel that resembled a boning knife, she carefully cut away all connections to the brain before gently lifting it out and placing it in a shiny steel tray. Another technician took it away to be weighed and the details added to the whiteboard.

Scott saw from the whiteboard that one cadaver had already been examined by Cara. The weights of the brain, heart, left and right lungs, liver, spleen and left and right kidneys had all been noted on the board.

He knew it wouldn't be long before the details of this victim were documented on that board as well. Another victim. Another set of statistics.

21

Cara moved around the cadaver, examining it once again before returning to her original position, citing some further observations for her records. She began by making a Y-shaped incision from the top of each shoulder. Because the cadaver was female, the Y shape was diverted beneath each breast. Cara took the incision down to the pubic bone.

Neil reached for a pair of silver long-handled shears that looked robust enough to cut branches in the garden. He passed them over to Cara, who cut through the rib cage; the sound of bone crunching bounced off every wall. The dense bone structure offered some resistance as Cara used both hands to break through each rib bone.

There were various methods that pathologists preferred when removing the contents of a cadaver's internal structures. Some preferred to take them out in several stages. Scott knew from their conversations that Cara liked to remove them in one piece before placing them in a yellow medical sack for examination at a later stage. This was commonly known as the Rokitansky method. She preferred this method because it minimised damage to the internal organs prior to inspection.

Scott watched in fascination as she carefully worked away around the body, like an artist working on their latest sculpture. He held a high degree of respect for those who worked in any mortuary. Cara told him once that "pathologists share a sense of curiosity, scientific interest and pleasure at being able to find the truth and share it."

Scott and Abby watched in equal measures of awe and revulsion as Cara made a small incision beneath the victim's chin just above the larynx, detaching the larynx and oesophagus from the pharynx. She then pulled the larynx and trachea downward, using her scalpel to free up the rest of the chest organs from their attachment at the spine.

The diaphragm was next on her hit list, and she cut it out of the body wall before pulling the abdominal organs out. Her last act was a single cut with her trusted scalpel, to the pelvic ligaments, bladder and rectum, which then allowed her and Neil to place the entire internal organ structure into a yellow sack.

Next, Cara examined the victim's fingers. "There's a lot of debris matter under her fingernails," she said, holding the victim's left hand and spreading out each digit to inspect them closely. "I'll take some sample scrapings from each and send them away for analysis to see if we've got any valuable evidence."

Scott nodded in agreement, hearing little, too distracted by Neil, who was using one of the soup ladles to extract blood and liquid matter that had collected in the bottom of the body cavity. He deftly scooped up the liquid, placing the contents of each ladle in a bucket he had positioned close by. Despite the many post-mortems Scott had been to, he would never get used to seeing a soup ladle being used in this way.

Cara's analysis of the body continued. Her hands disappeared in the body cavity before she moved on to the head and then worked her way down the body over the following hour.

Scott could see Abby becoming restless, and sensed she'd much rather be stuck behind a mountain of files back at her desk than observe this cadaver slowly being dismantled.

"I'm going to have some liver and bacon for dinner tonight... What are you going to have?" he asked, nudging her arm.

Abby's brows furrowed as she turned to look at Scott.

"Are you for real?" She shook her head and gestured to the body. "We've got soup ladles of blood, more splattered on the floor, entrails sitting over there in a yellow plastic bag, Cara elbow-deep in shit, and you're asking me what I'm having for dinner?"

Scott shrugged nonchalantly. "It's a reasonable enough question."

Abby offered no reply other than a slow shake of her head.

"When you kids have stopped fighting, you may want to know what my findings are so far," Cara interrupted.

"We are all ears," Scott assured her.

"Well, my initial findings are she died from a deep impact trauma to the head. Her skull is depressed in several areas, suggesting some blunt force trauma injury, which also led to heavy bleeding. There is no evidence of sexual interference than what we know already. No traces of other bodily fluids like semen either. Oh, and her nipples were removed after she'd died."

"Thanks, Cara," Scott said. "That's all we need to know at the moment. That gives us enough to go on. We need to head back to the office, so I'll await your full report later and leave you to it now if that's okay?"

Abby released a sigh of relief.

"Yep, it sure is." Cara smiled. "I'll catch you tonight?"

Scott nodded in embarrassment. On the way out, he avoided looking in Abby's direction, knowing that her teasing would soon follow.

22

"Catch you tonight, huh?" Abby teased again as they parked up. She'd pushed Scott for answers throughout their journey back but had been met with a deliberate wall of jovial silence.

Scott said nothing as he strode through the back door of the station.

"Got anything nice planned? Romantic dinner for two? Bunch of roses? Champagne?" she carried on.

"Enough! You're a bloody nightmare. I don't want to hear any more."

"She seems very keen on you. Well, that was the impression I got when I was having a cuppa with her."

Scott paused. Abby had his attention now. "Oh, really? What did she say?"

Abby tapped the side of her nose and marched ahead. "As you said, you don't want to hear any more."

"But..." Scott blurted out. He'd walked into that one.

As they made their way through the back of the station, the desk sergeant hollered down the corridor, "Baker, the DCI is looking for you."

Abby whispered, “Lucky you.”

Scott grumbled and shook his head. His phone rang.

“Is she in her office?” he asked the desk sergeant while glancing at his phone.

The sergeant nodded once to confirm.

Scott checked his phone properly and recognised the number as that of FLO Andrea Smith.

He answered it.

“Guv, do you still want me to bring Mr Newland to the station?” Andrea asked.

“Yes. We need to get a statement from him, and the quicker we build a timeline around the victim’s movements, the better.”

“I’m on my way with him now.” Andrea paused. “One thing of interest, guv. Mr Newland was looking through her personal effects. A watch he gave her was missing, a Dior watch, engraved on the back with ‘love Alan’.”

“Thanks. Speak soon.” He ended the call.

Abby was standing nearby.

“Abby, do me a favour, take Sian with you and get back over to the Newlands’. Ask around a few neighbours. Let’s get some background and history on the Newlands, and Christine in particular.”

She nodded.

“The husband’s on his way here with Andrea now. I’ll have another chat with him.”

23

When Scott arrived at DCI Jane Harvey's office, she was going through a report in her office whilst absent-mindedly singing to herself. The DCI was an unusual character and certainly not a stereotypical modern-day police officer. She was gritty, vocal and batty, confirmed traits from those who had worked with her. Her gruff voice and piercing stares intimidated even the toughest and most seasoned officers.

Rarely did anyone challenge her, including her spineless superior, Detective Superintendent John Meadows. He was six years her junior at forty-nine. In private, many officers blamed Meadows for DCI Harvey still being in post uncontested nor adequately supervised.

Scott interrupted her by clearing his throat. "Ma'am, you wanted to see me?"

Harvey continued to gaze at her report and hum. She waved him in and to take a seat.

Finally, she locked eyes with him. "How have you been recently?"

The question took Scott by surprise. He was fully

expecting a question about the current cases, but what she asked sounded a lot more personal. "I'm sorry, ma'am, I don't understand."

The DCI shrugged and raised her brows. "You seemed a little stressed at the briefing yesterday. I just wondered if something was on your mind, that's all." She stared at him inquisitively.

It was hard to read what the DCI was thinking. That was perhaps why so many other officers found her intimidating. Her neutral face was a closed book. Scott often wondered if he'd ever seen the real her, or if she was like this all the time.

"No, I'm good, ma'am. The team and I have a lot on our plate at the moment, and I'm sure, like me, you're keen to get results quickly. We're dealing with one or two slippery characters at the moment."

"How are we getting on there?" she asked, locking her fingers together on the desk. Her steely gaze was firmly fixed on him, causing Scott to shift uncomfortably in his seat.

"We've just had a positive ID on the woman we found last night. It looks like a blunt trauma injury to her head caused her death. I've got the husband coming in now to be interviewed, and hopefully he can shed some light on her background and movements. I've just dispatched Abby to the victim's street to ask around the neighbours to see if we can glean any information."

The DCI nodded approvingly. "And the girl, Libby?"

"Nothing further to add since the briefing last night, ma'am."

The DCI continued to nod, like one of those nodding dog toys that sat on the rear parcel shelf of a car.

"Okay, that will be all," she said. "Come and find me if you have further developments, but for now organise a team briefing before the close of business. Oh, and by the way,

Scott," she added, "if there's anything on your mind, my door is always open."

She returned her attention to the report.

Her parting comment and final action left Scott feeling a little unnerved.

Bemused, he rose slowly from the chair, not really sure why she'd called him there in the first place. He couldn't help but feel that there'd been a hidden agenda to their discussion, an agenda that he wasn't privy to.

Scott tried to shake off the niggling feeling that the DCI had been probing for something. He questioned whether it was something he'd said recently. Had someone reported his behaviour? Was she now questioning his efficiency?

Back in CID, Scott stopped at Raj's desk, where he helped himself to a French fondant fancy that Doughnut Boy had picked up that morning. It was only when the sickly stodge hit the bottom of his stomach that he realised he had eaten nothing since breakfast. The sugar rush gave him a headache. Convincing himself that a second fancy would miraculously soothe the orchestra of dull thuds inside his head, he helped himself again.

Raj swivelled around in his chair, taking him away from his computer.

"Raj, the victim found last night has been positively ID'd as Christine Newland. Abby's in the victim's neighbourhood, having a chat with a few neighbours. Mr Newland is downstairs waiting for me. I need you to do a bit of digging around. Do a background check on Christine Newland. Speak to her colleagues at work, her manager. Check if she had a social profile on Facebook. See if anything unusual has been happening to her over the last few weeks, okay?"

"Yep, I'm on it." He swivelled back and started furiously typing away on his keyboard.

Scott thought about Cara and their date tonight. He was

looking forward to seeing her. He sent her a quick text before his interview.

Hi, looking forward to seeing you tonight. Fancy some fish and chips for dinner?

He'd only taken a few more steps when his phone pinged back.

Boy, you know how to show a woman a good time!! Yep, sounds good, you cheapskate. Ramsden's at 7.30pm? x

He laughed as he hit reply.

LOL! Yes, see you there.

Cara had an ability he cherished: she could make him smile.

24

Alan Newland cast a lonely figure, his hands wrapped around a warm cup of tea. The family liaison officer PC Andrea Smith was by his side, giving him some words of reassurance, when Scott entered the room. Newland raised his head enough to acknowledge Scott's arrival. His eyes were narrowed, sore and red looking. It was as if he hadn't stopped crying since Scott had last seen him. He looked a shell of a man. His cheeks were gaunt, his hair a mess, his eyes staring blankly into his cup of tea. He might have been present in body, but Scott doubted he was there in mind.

"Mr Newland, I'm sorry for your loss, and I truly appreciate you taking the time to come in at what is a very difficult time. As you can hopefully appreciate, we're dealing with the tragic death of your wife, and the first twenty-four hours are absolutely crucial for us."

Alan Newland nodded wearily, without raising his head. "Why would anyone want to murder her?" he muttered, his lips barely parting to let the words out.

Scott didn't have an answer. He wished he did so he could

bring some resolution to end this man's pain and torture. "That's what we're trying to find out, Mr Newland, and any help or insights into your wife's movements or daily life would be really helpful."

For the first time since Scott had entered the room, Mr Newland raised his head properly. He stared for a moment into Scott's eyes. The man didn't have to say anything; the fear, anguish, loss and sheer confusion were written all over his face.

Scott explained why the interview would be recorded before asking, "Mr Newland, was there any change in your wife's behaviour recently?"

"No, nothing," he replied.

"Did she seem herself when you last saw her?"

"Yes, she seemed fine. She just went about her normal routine first thing in the morning. She gave Lucy a kiss goodbye before she left. She'd even made my packed lunch as normal." A small smile softened his face as he stared at the table.

"Did she mention anything about having any problems or arguments with anyone else or someone at work?"

"Not as far as I was aware. She was a feisty, gutsy woman at the best of times, but I never knew of anyone she'd fallen out with. She hardly had a bad word to say about anyone." He slowly shook his head.

Scott watched Alan Newland for any signs of him holding back information. So far, the man seemed genuine, but he needed to probe further.

"Mr Newland, were you and your wife having any difficulties as a couple?"

The insinuation seemed to both upset and confuse the man. He looked up at Scott, not knowing exactly what to say in response. "No, nothing like that," he said, furiously shaking his head. "We love... loved each other. Same as any couple, you have the occasional disagreement about things like buying too much shopping in Sainsbury's, or the expensive Next credit card bill. Don't all couples have those types of disagreements?"

Scott continued, "What were your movements on the day that she went missing?"

Newland's eyes narrowed. "Are you suggesting I had anything to do with this?"

"Mr Newland, we're trying to ascertain her last movements and whether anything out of the ordinary happened on that particular day. Anything that could give us an indication as to the reason behind her death. We have to explore all avenues for completeness, so if you could just answer the question, that would be helpful."

"I left home about eight forty-five a.m. and drove straight to my office. I was there all day until late afternoon. My secretary can vouch for that."

"Just one other question, do you have any friends or relatives close to Hove Park that might explain why she was there or the near vicinity?"

Newland shook his head in despair.

Scott had the feeling he would not glean any further information about the final moments in Christine's life from her husband.

He wrapped up the interview, thanking Mr Newland for his time and asking him to remain at home in case they had further news for him.

25

"Everyone listen up, please," Scott said to his team in the briefing room. "The investigation into the death of Libby Stevens has uncovered a much wider problem. There is a realistic possibility we're dealing with domestic trafficking of underage girls for sex." He paused for a moment, casting his eyes around the room. The numbers had swelled to more than double due to the addition of officers linked to units involved with intelligence gathering and the safeguarding of vulnerable children and adults.

With the scale of the offences uncovered, it warranted extra resources being drafted in and the sharing of information. Scott felt a personal desire to stop this awful trade in young, vulnerable children. That was all they were in his eyes: defenceless, impressionable children exploited by sick, depraved individuals. It was natural to assume that the majority of offenders would be male, but in Scott's time as an officer, he had come across women who were just as twisted and vile.

As usual, DCI Harvey sat at the top end of the long oval table. Her expressionless eyes gave nothing away, but she stopped and glanced at each one of the members in turn. It was apparent that she was weighing up each of them.

Scott continued, "We think young British girls are being targeted, groomed and abused, and then moved around the country by organised gangs. We need to liaise with other regional forces to identify the scale of the problem. In particular, Manchester and Birmingham because of what we've gleaned so far about the missing girls."

"Anywhere else in particular, guv?" Sian asked.

"I'd also suggest major cities like Cardiff, Liverpool and Glasgow, too."

"Have these gangs got formal links?"

"We don't think so, Sian. I believe they just link together as and when they need to, but that's to be confirmed. The key is to identify the big players. We have Johnny Wright in the frame; he's linked with the most recent target, Jenna Wade. She has been returned to Benedict's residential unit and is back in school again."

"How many girls are we talking about here?" asked a portly, middle-aged male officer from the vulnerability unit.

Scott turned to the whiteboard and proceeded to tap on each image pinned to the board. "We're not entirely sure, but we know of at least four who are currently involved in this. We have Libby Stevens, aged fifteen from Brighton, found dead on the beach. Jasmine Reed, aged fifteen from Brighton, found dead in Birmingham. Rishi Mehta, aged fifteen from Manchester, alive and believed to be in Sussex, possibly Brighton, and Jenna Wade, aged fourteen from Brighton. Some are from residential units, which is why I believe they've been targeted. They're easy prey. Others have been reported missing but have slipped through the net."

A thin, bespectacled female officer from the vulnerability unit shifted in her chair before adding to the conversation. "Where does the trafficking come into it?"

Scott replied, "Intelligence suggests that once the girls have been sexually exploited to such an extent that they are no longer fresh meat, they're moved to another city, where the whole process starts again. Raj and Sian, first thing tomorrow, I want you to liaise with our colleagues in Manchester, Birmingham, Cardiff, Liverpool and Glasgow to begin with. See what intel they can share with us and then feed it back to the vulnerability unit, too." Scott turned to Mike. "I want you to look at local men who are on the sex offender's register, anyone we can squeeze for information. Many of them have their noses to the ground and can give us a head start."

Mike, who was chewing the end of his Bic pen, stopped. "We know of one guy, Robert Shaw, a real sick paedo. I remember nicking him some time ago. He preferred girls in their teens, so I think it's worth paying him a visit. If I remember correctly, he's been caught near youth clubs before. Bit of a loopy case. He's got mental health issues... think some type of personality disorder." He scratched his head, and his expression tightened, as if searching for details from memory.

Scott nodded. "Sounds good, get an update on his current location, and we'll pay him a visit tomorrow morning."

With no further questions from the team, Scott concluded the briefing. After, he dealt with the most pressing emails in his inbox and double-checked the press release going out the following day on Christine Newland.

He was switching off his PC when Abby poked her head around the door.

"Hot date with the scalpel queen tonight?" she teased.

Scott gave a small smirk to acknowledge her taunt. "Yes, we're heading out for dinner."

His response took him by surprise. It was the first time he'd referred to their relationship without hesitation or extra thought. Perhaps Cara was having a better influence on him than he cared to admit.

Scott continued, “As my DS and therefore my deputy SIO, I’ll leave everything in your more than capable hands.” He splayed his hands out. “That means if the shit hits the fan, you’re on your own.”

Abby narrowed her eyes, looking unsure as to whether he was being serious. As a deputy senior investigating officer, she’d take the lead on the cases the team were investigating. It would be her call on what action to take – something he knew she looked forward to, whilst being shit-scared at the prospect.

“Seriously?” she asked with a hint of curiosity and concern.

He laughed, leaning back in his chair. “Seriously. But facing the wrath of the DCI isn’t something I’d wish on my worst enemy.” He winked at her. “Call me if you need to.”

Abby mockingly wiped her brow and exhaled. “Phew! Go and enjoy yourself, you deserve it.”

26

It was a cool summer's evening as Scott stood outside Harry Ramsden's restaurant opposite Palace Pier. The town was still buzzing. Commuters had been replaced with those heading out for a piece of the local nightlife.

Scott watched the traffic slow to a crawl at the small roundabout in front of him. Each driver then played Russian roulette, glancing left and right before pulling out. The Highway Code etiquette was thrown to the wind, and frequent thumps on car horns from frustrated and impatient drivers followed.

"Hello, young man."

The words broke the hypnotic spell he was under.

Scott turned, expecting to find Cara, but startled to see a blonde, big-chested woman. The woman in her early thirties was wearing a knee-length skirt, black knee-length boots and a blouse, with the first few buttons undone. Her makeup looked as if it had been put on in the dark with a garden shovel.

She drawled. "If you're looking for business, I can give you an amazing time. How about you buy me a drink?" Her deep-throated voice sounded like it had been ravaged by cigarettes. She chewed loudly on a piece of gum as she looked him up and down provocatively.

He played along. "What else did you have in mind?"

"Anything you want, lover. You can have anything... for a price."

He could arrest her for soliciting right now, but he could do without the aggravation. Plus it would spoil his evening.

Scott pulled out his warrant card and shoved it at her. "Take this as a friendly caution. I suggest you go home, put your feet up and enjoy a hot chocolate. If I see you out again tonight, I'll nick you for soliciting – your choice." He raised an eyebrow.

The colour drained from her pale, pasty, puffy face. The chewing sound was replaced with an uncomfortable grinding of teeth.

She rolled her eyes and turned, but not before she delivered a parting comment. "Wanker."

As Scott watched her march away, he saw Cara walking towards him, a curious look on her face. She exchanged a glance with the blonde, buxom woman as she passed.

"You two-timing me?" she teased Scott, still looking confused.

"No, just doing my bit of friendly neighbourhood policing," he replied. He held the door open for her and followed Cara inside.

The pair hungrily tucked into a large portion of cod and chips. Their evening began where their last date had ended, full of laughter and cheek. Scott was still getting used to the idea of just how easy it was in Cara's company. She was fun, flirty, intelligent and attractive.

Oh so attractive.

Tonight was no exception. Cara's long, flowing dark hair tumbled over her shoulders. She wore an off-the-shoulder, thin light beige jumper that hinted subtle sex appeal. Her tight jeans were finished off with black heeled shoes.

Scott had never seen her have an off clothes day. Even in her clinical green scrubs, Cara exuded a sexual magnetism.

Feeling full, Scott suggested they head over to the pier for a stroll.

27

Leaning up against the white railings, they took a moment to soak up the vibrancy of the pier, the beach and the falling sun. Looking out along the seafront, Scott could see a fair few people still milling around. Some sat on picnic blankets, enjoying al fresco dining. Another group stood on the edge of the beach, taking bets as to who could stand their ground the longest before the waves reached their feet. Some poor sod lost the gamble, much to the squeals of laughter from those around him.

They even watched a dog run in and out of the surf, jumping with delight as each wave washed over.

Cara turned to Scott. "You having a nice time?"

"I'm having a lovely time," he replied, hunched over the railing, looking at the dark, murky, swirling water below. "It's nice to get away from all the grief of work, to be honest. A bit of sanity in this mad world."

Cara nodded. "That current case with the girl must be hard?"

Scott nodded once, his thoughts sailing in the wind,

much like the surrounding seagulls, which hung effortlessly in the air, just out of reach.

She nudged him in the ribs. "Well, the night's not over, so let's go have some fun."

With that she turned and was already halfway to the arcade beneath the large neon Palace Pier sign. Scott ran to catch up.

The arcade was awash with the sound of chatter from the throng of tourists frittering away their money on the numerous racing car rides. Scott was greeted by a cacophony of sound from all directions as flashing lights, spinning dials, the sounds of tumbling coins and musical tones lit up the machines.

As he looked around, he could see this was nothing more than a den of soft gambling. A hypnotic place where very few won anything of substance, but it drew people in. Unsuspecting punters were willing to part with their cash in the slim hope of winning a handful of small change or a worthless small toy.

He and Cara cashed up a twenty-pound note and split it into two cups. Over the next hour, they moved from one machine to another, trying their luck. The occasional win lifted their spirits and egged them on further. It didn't stop their cash reserves dwindling rapidly as they got drawn into throwing more coins down the hungry throats of machines. The very same machines that had stood the test of time entertaining generations over the years.

After losing all his money, Scott came to Cara's side. She was engrossed in a coin drop game. Concentration was etched on her face. She wanted to win; she needed to win.

He watched as she dropped one two-pence coin in the slot. It bounced from one pin to another before finally coming to rest on the platform alongside dozens of coins perched precariously on the edge. Just one coin in the right spot would tip them, and Cara was determined to be the victor. She dropped her coins at regular intervals, her eyes fixated on the prize, not averting her gaze for a moment in case she missed something.

In that moment he was drawn to Cara. Her energy for life, exuding from every pore of her body, brought a warm glow to his dark world and made him smile.

A loud squeal broke his daze. Cara erupted into an excited frenzy as she fist-pumped the air.

"I won!" she screeched before singing, "I'm in the money, I'm in the money," and jigging her shoulders in delight. She reached down to scoop up her hard-fought earnings.

Scott laughed and shook his head. He estimated that in the time he'd stood by this machine, she'd spent three pounds in two-pence pieces. Staring into her cup, she'd won the princely sum of thirty-six pence in coins.

After claiming her spoils, they walked back along the seafront to the Regency Square car park. Even amongst the throng of people and cars, they still had time to enjoy a pleasant and relaxing walk.

Cara finally broke the comfortable silence between them. "I had a lovely time."

"Me too," Scott replied, pausing for a moment. "You're pretty amazing, you know that?"

Cara smirked. "Hmm, yes, I know. Aren't you a lucky boy?"

"I am, in more ways than you could ever know." He leant in and gave her the softest kiss.

As he pulled away, Scott felt something that had been missing for many years.

Happiness.

28

The property that Scott and Mike were visiting this morning sat near the back of the Whitehawk Estate, a sprawling development of council housing. For those who didn't know their way around, it was easy to get lost in the warren of small streets with identical-looking terraced dwellings. Scott felt a certain degree of sympathy for anyone who unwittingly took a wrong turn and found themselves deep inside the belly of the estate. It was bad enough turning up during the day, but he knew that at night, the deserted streets and estate took on a more intimidating and chilling existence.

They pulled up outside a row of four terraced houses, each one staggered back slightly from its neighbour to the right. A large satellite dish was on the outside wall of each property. A standard brown wooden door and white UPVC windows added to the bland feel of the area. Short green iron railings more suited to a park or recreation ground kept the overgrown garden from claiming some of the pavement.

As they approached the front gate, Scott noticed a few kids playing on the grass in the small playground provided for local families. The sight left an uneasy feeling in Scott's stomach that gnawed away at him. The kids were far too close to have gone unnoticed by the resident they were here to see.

They heard Robert Shaw before they saw him. From behind the overgrown bushes that obscured part of the garden, they found him on his knees, muttering loudly to himself. He was turning over the soil and picking out weeds around the few shrubs and plants that he had. The majority of his garden was laid with patio slabs, making it a low-maintenance space. He looked up as the pair stood over him; his back was hunched over, his hair messy to match the unkempt beard.

Shaw stared at them nervously, licking his dry lips, hesitation in his movements as he looked around to see who was watching.

"What you lot doing here?" he whispered. "I don't want to be seen talking to you."

"The feeling is mutual," Mike said. He spoke to Shaw through gritted teeth. "You have a string of offences against young girls, and we need to talk to you about a case we're dealing with." He bent down and looked Shaw right in the eyes.

There was no love lost between Shaw and the DC; their paths had crossed many times. Scott knew Mike despised grown men who preyed on vulnerable children. He was just a tinderbox waiting to explode if the likes of Shaw or his conspirators antagonised him.

Shaw recoiled and straightened his thin bony frame, his oversized clothes hanging off him.

In a hushed tone, he pointed a finger at both of them and spat, "I told you, that's all in the past now. I've done my time. Yes... yes... yes."

"That's okay, is it?" Mike fired back, hatred evident in his eyes.

Scott looked around at the surrounding houses. "We can talk to you out here and give the curtain twitchers some meaty gossip, or we can do this inside."

Shaw spun on his heel and strode inside, muttering incoherently, Scott and Mike a few steps behind.

Off the hallway of this two-up two-down was a small, sparsely furnished lounge. As Scott peered in, he saw a small television sitting on a milk crate. Positioned a few feet away was a well-worn, purple two-seater sofa beneath the front window, and a stack of old newspapers scattered in a pile beside it. The green carpet was threadbare in places, and the whole room had a heavy smell of tobacco. Yellow staining on the ceiling suggested that the place hadn't been decorated in many years.

These houses were provided by Brighton and Hove council. The only obligation was to provide tenants with adequate accommodation, not furnish it. With Shaw's record, it was probable the door closed on most jobs he applied for. State handouts and handyman work were likely his only means of support.

Shaw stood behind his dirty net curtain, shifting from one foot to the other, peering out nervously.

"They can't see me; no one can see me," he muttered.

Mike crossed his arms and continued, "I don't know why you're worried, no one around here knows we're police officers, and no one knows who you are."

Shaw swallowed hard. "Well, I wanna keep it that way, you plank."

"Of course if we wanted to announce ourselves and alert the neighbours, we could have turned up in a squad car. I'm sure that would raise a few questions and make things very *awkward* for you. We wouldn't want that, would we?" As Mike paused, Shaw became further agitated.

Scott casually walked around the room, taking in the bland surroundings. "Speaking of questions, we have one for you: where would someone need to go in Brighton to have sex with... *underage girls*?" He turned and fixed his stare on Shaw; the man squirmed underneath his steely gaze.

Shaw ran a hand through his thick greasy hair, alarm written over his face. He was breathing erratically, swallowing hard, his eyes darting in all directions. He crossed his arms defensively. "Are you joking me?"

Scott and Mike continued to watch him. Scott knew from their extensive interview training that silence was a great asset. It made those on the receiving end increasingly nervous and often led them to say things they'd normally keep to themselves, just to break the silence.

Shaw shrugged nervously. "I don't know. I told you it's all in the past for me."

"Johnny Wright a friend of yours?"

Shaw stared at the floor, playing with an imaginary football between his feet. "Never heard of him."

Scott continued, "I thought you would have since he offers young girls to people like you. We need to know where he offers them."

Shaw's hands were clenched tight by his sides. "I don't know!" he said, his voice rising. "I swear."

"Stop holding back, Shaw," Mike snarled. He strode forward and came nose to nose with the man. He grabbed him by his shirt.

Scott stepped in between the two men. Scott gave Mike a warning look to cool it. His DC was treading a fine line between turning up the heat and being on the receiving end of a disciplinary. Mike stepped back but continued to glare at him.

A shaken Shaw adjusted his shirt. "That's assault, you know! Everyone deserves a second chance. If I could help, I would."

Rather than risk a formal complaint being levelled at one of his officers, Scott took over. "That might be so, but young abused girls don't get one. I wonder what your neighbours would think of your second chance?"

Shaw panicked even further, his breathing coming fast and short, his eyes wide and wild with fear.

"Okay, okay, I don't know where, but I know a guy who said that if I was ever interested, which by the way I'm not, to give him a shout. I can call him now?"

29

Having got the information from Shaw, Scott and Mike drove back to the station in silence for most of the way. As they approached the back entrance, Scott parked by the door.

He turned to his DC. "Mike, don't pull a stunt like that again... Do I make myself clear?"

"Understood, guv. I'm sorry. Scrotes like that need to be taught a lesson. Back in the forces, we dished out our discipline to sort out our problems. I can't help myself sometimes."

"Well, you're not in the army any more. You and I need a chat after this case is over. If you do that again, your career isn't going to go far."

They headed inside, and Scott mustered the team together around Raj's desk for a quick update. He perched on the edge of Raj's desk, pushing aside empty food wrappings in frustration. Raj shifted uncomfortably in his chair, choosing to look anywhere but at Scott.

Scott said, "Right, we've got a possible lead in the Libby

Stevens and trafficking case. Robert Shaw gave us a name and an address in Crestway. He said a man by the name of Ardit Gashi is running a house where they have up to four teenage girls available for sex. Whether they're still there or not, we're not sure. They tend to move around a lot to avoid raising suspicion. I'll assign officers to head to the house to observe until we can move in."

The team nodded as Scott recalled the visit to Shaw. There was a buzz and renewed vigour amongst those gathered. Finally, they were making some inroads into a case that they all felt fully committed to resolving.

"Sian, Raj, anything to add?" Scott asked.

Sian excitedly reached for her notes. "Yes, guv. We've made a connection between Brighton and Birmingham. Our colleagues in Birmingham have intelligence that the trafficking of girls is being run by an Albanian called Ramiz Hajdari. He was known to be associated with Jasmine Reed shortly before she died. He's done some time for extortion, pimping and the supply of drugs. When he was arrested last time, his phone traffic showed a lot of communications between himself and your man Ardit Gashi."

Those huddled around the desk muttered excitedly. This was just a small piece of the jigsaw, but a crucial one nevertheless, especially if there was a threat to life. That meant time wasn't on their side. In the meantime, Scott needed his team to continue intelligence gathering. Find victims willing to talk. Only then could a strong enough case be built. They needed facts.

Sian continued, "We also had Manchester confirm that their suspect is another Albanian, Murat Ahmeti. They've not been able to nail him for anything; he's been too clever at covering his tracks with multiple layers to his set-up. Gang members who've been caught so far have been small fry, taking the fall for the big boys. But, again, phone records show messages sent between him, Ardit and Ramiz."

Raj added, "Do you think that Jenna Wade knows anything about the wider operation?"

Scott shook his head. "I doubt it. Jenna refuses to believe she's part of this process. She's convinced Johnny loves her. He's given her the kind of affection she's never experienced in her life. So much so that in a few weeks' time when he asks her to sleep with other men as a favour to him, she'll probably do it. Before she knows it, she'll be addicted to drugs, dumped by Johnny and introduced to a wider network of sexual predators in Manchester or Birmingham."

"What now?" Mike asked.

"We've got the address Shaw gave us in the Crestway. Abby, organise and brief a tactical entry team to meet us there. I'll update the DCI so she's aware of what we're about to do."

His DS nodded.

"Raj, can you pull up an aerial view of the property on Google Maps?"

Raj did, which allowed the team to study the location and plan their approach.

Scott leant in and pointed to a spot on the map. "This is the property we are targeting. It looks like it's in the middle of a row of terraced houses, so entry and exit points will only be front and back." He pointed to a patch of open land behind the property. "There's a potential escape route right there. Abby, arrange for a dog unit to cover the rear. It looks like they can get there through Hinton Close." He traced his finger from the house to the green-grass area.

Abby nodded once. "When are we going?"

"In the next thirty minutes – timing is crucial. I've got uniform sitting with Shaw at the moment to stop him from warning them about our arrival. Any other news?" Scott asked, looking around at those gathered.

Raj cleared his throat. "Whilst we're here and I remember, the enquiries have come back clean so far on the Newland case. Christine was well respected at work by her boss and colleagues. Always punctual, spoke about her family often. She had a Facebook profile, posted once a week or so, and had thirty-four Facebook friends I'll start working through. The only thing out of character was when she raced off after receiving a call about twelve thirty p.m. She grabbed her bag, told her boss her daughter wasn't feeling well, and she needed to pick her up."

"And did she?"

"No, guv. Her daughter's school confirmed that Lucy was in school all day."

Scott nodded his approval. "Good job, Raj, keep me informed on anything further. The press appeal has gone out today, so you should get a response from the public hopefully. You and Sian can man the phone lines. Did we manage to find out who called her, or the number she called?"

Raj nodded. "The call was made to her place of work. Switchboard could only confirm that it was a male voice. The call log for their system confirmed a mobile number. The mobile number isn't registered, and there's no answer when you dial it."

Abby raised her pen. "I went to see Jenna Wade again today. She was caught sneaking out of school to meet Johnny Wright, who was waiting for her at the gates. He rang earlier to meet her. He said he wanted to see her because it was important."

"Important? What's so important suddenly? What did he say?" Scott replied. He narrowed his eyes and pinched his chin.

"He just told her he wanted her to meet some friends. I

tried to get her to open up. I thought she may have been holding back, but she's a stubborn cow. In the end I gave her my card and told her to call me if she wanted to talk."

The team exchanged nervous glances. Scott knew it too. Jenna was about to be moved to the next stage of the traffickers' plan.

30

Scott, Abby and Mike left the station in convoy for Hollingdean, followed by the tactical entry team and a dog unit. His adrenaline was pumping. The team was on edge, and the urgency to get a result was clearly at the forefront of their minds.

As the vehicle turned into the Crestway, the driver switched to a silent approach. The last thing Scott wanted was to announce their arrival and tip off those in the house.

The driver parked, and the convoy was positioned a short distance from the property in Thompson Road. Scott commanded his team to wait whilst they waited for the dog unit to take up its place at the rear of the property. There was a small parade of shops opposite the target house, which meant there were more members of the public milling around than Scott would have liked.

In any situation such as this, the first thing he needed to ensure was the safety of the public during the raid on the house. From the position of the house in proximity to the shops, Scott was confident that the public would be a sufficient distance away not to come into harm's way.

Scott took a deep breath. He wasn't sure what they'd find inside. He was hoping to find some girls as well as the men controlling them. If anyone decided to make a run for it from the back of the property, they'd come face-to-face with a forty-kilo German shepherd police dog racing towards them at twenty-five miles per hour. You'd either have to be very brave or very stupid to take on a trained police dog.

Scott's phone chimed at the arrival of a new message. He checked his phone, pleased to see it was Cara asking him out for dinner tonight. Just seeing her name on his phone filled the emptiness with a warm glow. The fact she was asking *him* out for dinner flattered him.

He thought for a moment about a suitable response, knowing it was time to take their relationship to the next level. He hesitated for a few seconds before hitting the reply button.

Dinner tonight, 8 p.m. at mine?

Her reply came swiftly.

Yes.

Scott gave her his address in Rutland Gardens and signed off with:

Can't talk, on an op. x

Can't wait. xx

He pocketed his phone and concentrated on the task ahead. Prior to their arrival, officers watching the property had reported that a male had entered about thirty minutes earlier and was just leaving the property when Scott and the team arrived. Scott concluded that it was a punter and requested that officers pick him up on suspicion of sex with a minor once he was out of sight of the house.

The strike had been organised for two p.m. With five minutes to go, the urgency to move was tangible. Silence prevailed in the car; the outside noise was drowned out by the throbbing pulse in Scott's head. The sun, streaming in through the windows, had raised the temperature inside the car.

"I'm sweltering in this tin can!" Mike fumed to no one in particular. His comment was met with stony silence from Scott and Abby.

Scott keyed his radio. "Two minutes – everyone in position and ready to go?"

"Confirmed, guv," came two replies, one from the tactical team situated in front of them and another from the dog unit. Scott shifted in his seat, the anti-stab vest hampering his movements and making everything unbearably hot. His shirt stuck to his back.

With one minute to go, Scott looked at Abby and Mike. "You two ready?"

They both nodded, keen to get on with the raid.

As the second hand hit twelve, Scott gave the command.

"Go, go, go."

The van in front grunted into action and moved off at speed, turning left into the Crestway, with Scott's vehicle on their tail. Abby and Mike held on to a grab handle with one hand, the other on a door handle, ready to exit when they stopped. The adrenaline coursed through Scott's veins. His muscles tightened as he gripped the wheel hard, his whole body taut and ready for action. His heart pounded, threatening to burst through his chest.

The commotion of them pulling up caused a few

onlookers to stop and stare. Both vehicles emptied in seconds, with all nine officers racing to the front door.

Scott and his team stood aside as a burly tactical entry officer led the way. He had “the red enforcer”, a sixteen-kilogramme steel battering ram that officers used to gain entry into properties. Two other officers followed him, equipped with a sledgehammer and go bar, which resembled an oversized crowbar.

The wooden door and frame offered little resistance. It splintered and collapsed when more than three tonnes of kinetic energy smashed through it. The door flew off its hinges, and the remaining uniformed officers poured through the opening, trampling over the debris, shouting, “Police! Stay where you are.”

The team dispersed in all directions.

Mike followed some of the officers through the ground floor as they made their way from room to room, shouting, “Clear,” when they found nothing. Scott and Abby thundered up the steps with three officers, who scoured the first-floor rooms.

Scott’s attention was drawn to commotion coming from a back room. Officers were shouting, “Get down, get the fuck down!”

As he reached the room, Scott saw officers dragging a man back in who had been trying to escape through an open window. He was an overweight, scruffily dressed man in a grey jumper, dirty blue jeans and burgundy leather jacket and had opted to run the gauntlet with the canine rather than take on the two officers racing towards him. Fortunately for him, he was being wrestled to the ground before being searched and cuffed with a cable tie.

“Good job, lads,” shouted Scott as he strode towards them.

He knelt down as the man’s face contorted with anger.

Spittle erupted from the man's mouth as he screamed obscenities at being restrained.

Scott kept his cool. "I'm arresting you on the suspicion of the control of a prostitute for monetary gains; you do not have to say anything, but it may harm your defence if you do not mention, when questioned, something which you rely on in court. Anything you do say can be given in evidence... Now get this shit out of here."

31

Scott stood, sidetracked for a moment, as his team hauled the man away.

Abby called out from farther down the hallway, "We've got another one, guv."

He headed into the hallway and found Abby in a room on the opposite side of the landing. She was perched on the end of a bed, her arm around a thin, emaciated girl no older than fifteen or sixteen. Scott's emotions swirled inside him like a turbulent winter storm; a mixture of sadness and anger collided with a sense of relief.

Judging from her thin, scraggly, gaunt face and her sunken eyes framed in dark circles, she could have passed for as young as twelve or thirteen. Abby looked up at Scott, a look of revulsion and despair written over her face. As a mother, her maternal instincts were kicking in. She stroked the girl's untidy, greasy hair.

Abby quietly mouthed at Scott, "Kelly from Manchester," while the girl stared at the carpet.

Her thin white blouse, loosely done up with two buttons, showed off her naked small breasts underneath. Her short black miniskirt wrapped tightly around her pale bruised thighs, showing the lengths her captors had gone to, to make her look older.

Scott's anger threatened to consume him. His objectivity was fast being replaced with red mist. He wanted to head out and deliver a *different* kind of justice on the prisoner they'd detained.

Evil scum.

Scott dragged his gaze away from the trembling girl sitting on the bed to Mike standing in the hallway. His narrowed eyes, fixed on the girl, told Scott that he was likely imagining the vile acts that had gone on in this dingy, dark bedroom. The carpet was dirty and stained – with what horrors Scott could only imagine. A pungent, musty smell hung in the air, assaulting his senses. A solitary double bed was the only furniture in the room; a small plastic bin by the side of the bed contained tissues and used condoms. Blue curtains hung loosely from a pine curtain rail, shielding the outside world from the abuse that took place in the room.

The entire property was degrading. Unpainted plastered walls, dark wooden doors, bare frames and skirtings. What little carpet covered the dirty floors had been left to rot, just like the rest of the house.

Scott walked up to Mike and tapped him on the shoulder. "You okay?"

Mike just nodded, anger etched into his face, gritting his teeth. He pointed towards an adjoining room, where another officer stood.

As Scott peered into the next room, he inhaled sharply at what he saw.

On a double bed lay another girl, each hand secured to the bed frame with handcuffs, her tiny wrists red with painful welts showing she'd struggled. Her eyes were partially closed.

Scott couldn't determine whether she was unconscious,

drugged, fatigued or choosing to blot out her experiences. Another officer from the entry team was already cutting her free with bolt cutters. Scott walked into the room and knelt beside her.

Shit, another poor soul.

Mike stood over Scott's shoulder, sighing. "I want to run the fuckers down, put them in a room with me and make them breathe their last breath."

He must have read Scott's mind.

"You're safe now," Scott whispered to the semiconscious girl. "I'm Scott. I'm with the police. What's your name?"

The girl's eyes flickered as she attempted to focus. Scott gently wiped her sweaty, long blonde dirty hair off her face. Her cheeks were red and sore, her eyes were a dull distant blue, which no doubt had once sparkled in happier times. Her face was pale and lifeless. The worry and sadness of being thrust into this life had robbed her.

The girl parted her cracked lips, her mouth dry. She gently mouthed, "Sabina."

Judging from the tone of her accent, Scott suspected she wasn't from the UK.

"Sabina, we're here to help you. How old are you, and where are you from?"

She took a few moments to lick her lips. Scott quietly asked Mike to get her water whilst he waited for her to answer. He turned his attention back to the helpless child lying there. Sabina's eyes remained unfocused. Perhaps she was deliberately choosing to switch off, to avoid the pain and loneliness she must have endured.

"I'm Sabina Lunga. I'm fifteen… from Albania."

Shit!

The reality hit Scott, and he bowed his head. This had turned from domestic trafficking and prostitution to an internationally organised crime ring.

32

Scott leant back in a chair in custody while the suspect was booked in. He'd handed the property over to scenes-of-crime officers who'd be combing through the bedrooms, gathering up the dirty, bloodied and semen-stained sheets, as well as the used condoms. With any luck, there'd be sufficient DNA evidence to allow them to identify those who had visited.

Scott needed a few moments to calm down and compose himself. Even though they'd had a good result and detained a key suspect, Ardit Gashi, Scott and the rest of the team felt a sense of shock and deflation.

His thoughts were interrupted by a commotion at the custody desk as officers wrestled with Ardit Gashi. His protestations and aggression were met with physical restraint as the officers pinned him to the floor.

Scott strode towards the man, stopping inches from Gashi, who continued to wriggle and attempt to break free from the officers. He stared at Gashi with an anger that simmered under the surface, ready to explode.

"Who do you think you are?"

"What you on about?" Gashi replied in broken English.

"Just calm down, and stop resisting whilst we process you," Scott snarled.

Gashi smiled and spat in Scott's direction. "I have done nothing."

Scott lunged forward and dropped a knee onto Ghasi's back.

The man yelled and squirmed on the floor.

DCI Harvey surprised Scott by stepping in to defuse the situation.

She nodded to an empty room. "In here, now!" she barked at Scott. He entered the room, and she closed the door behind them.

Harvey crossed her arms. "I think you need to take a moment to calm down. Emotions are running high here, Scott. I know how important this case is, but you need to take it easy, okay? You're a bloody good officer. Don't screw it up by losing your rag." She raised both brows. "You got a good result today; focus on that. This won't be the first or last where a suspect winds you up. You need to remain focused and professional at all times. Any officer who saw what you saw today would be affected, no doubt about it. But I stress that you need to *keep a lid on it*, for your sake."

Scott glared at his DCI. She was right, but he couldn't stop the anger from surfacing. He knew his emotions were clouding his judgement, and he was running close to the wrong side of the line.

The poor girls... the poor, poor girls.

His humanity, his need to seek justice for these girls was clouding his judgement. He blamed it for his behaviour.

"Do you understand?" Harvey added.

Scott walked to the door.

"Yes," he replied before slamming the door behind him.

33

Both victims were checked over by the police doctor, Kelly more cooperative than Sabina. With social services now involved, Scott could get on with the task of extracting vital information and evidence to blow this case apart.

Whilst Scott completed the paperwork, the rest of the team ran a series of critical interviews. Abby and Raj had already started to interview victim Kelly Southall. Abby agreed to join Scott after to interview Sabina Lunga. Mike and Sian would be interviewing Ardit Gashi.

The safe suite was a specially designed area within the station where victims of rape and sexual assault were interviewed in privacy and comfort. It was less formal than other parts of the station that might appear uninviting or intimidating for victims. The space had comfortable armchairs, sofas and cushions, potted plants. Colourful wall prints and soft tones of blue wall paint offered a more calming and reassuring environment.

Sabina was dressed in a paper suit. Her clothes had been removed for forensic analysis. To Scott she looked scared, her thin frame shaking slightly. She looked numb, her eyes telling a story of hatred, and misery.

Abby and Scott sat in separate armchairs. A social worker sat with Sabina. She was a middle-aged woman with short, slightly wild brown hair, and tinted wide-framed glasses. She reminded Scott of a younger Maureen Lipman. Her narrow lips, blank expression and thin face made her look cold and unsympathetic. It was likely she'd been in this situation many times, to the extent that the process no longer fazed her.

The interview with Sabina was crucial for their investigation. They could gain invaluable insight into the operation and bring down the key players.

Scott said, "Sabina, you're in protective custody now, and you're safe. We will be recording this interview on video; is that okay with you?"

He looked at her, willing her to cooperate, but she said nothing.

Abby leant forward, her hands cupped together. "I heard you didn't want to cooperate with the doctor. He's just trying to help you."

The victim stared at the wall opposite her. Then, in broken English, she said, "I'm not sick. I don't need help."

Abby nodded. "We want to make sure you're okay, that's all."

Scott could see Sabina was paralysed with fear, but she held her nerve.

"It's none of your business," she whispered, looking at Abby. She returned to her fixed stare.

Scott noticed that when she spoke, her words seemed cold and disconnected. It felt like he was looking at her through a pane of glass – her eyes were veiled, the smooth lines of her face not showing much emotion.

No doubt a defence mechanism of her subconscious to help her cope.

What surprised him was the dissonance between what she was saying and the way she was saying it. It was as though the only way she could get the sentences out was to be as calm and matter-of-fact as possible.

"We're here to help, Sabina. We want to catch the people who did this to you. We want to make sure that no one else falls into their hands. Will you help?" Scott asked, almost pleading.

The silence felt like hours had passed when in reality it was less than a minute or two.

Sabina offered a small nod.

Scott sighed in relief. "Why don't you start from the beginning, eh?"

"My mother sold me to man who sent me here. She couldn't cope... me and my two sisters too much to look after. No money in our town in Albania. He gave me passport and paid for me to come to UK with him."

"Who? Did he have a name?"

She shook her head. "Just a man... but he called other man Ardit often... called him brother. He only comes here sometimes. He was leaving me and taking an Indian girl back."

Scott shot Abby a quick glance, who nodded slightly.

"He brought me here," she continued, nodding towards the window. "He gave me to Ardit. He then gave me to Johnny... Johnny looked after me."

Scott bit his lip; the more Sabina talked, the more implicit Johnny became in this seedy operation.

There's no way you're wriggling out of this one, matey.

Sabina looked down at the table, wringing her hands beneath it. "He treated me well. I believed him. I loved him, and he loved me straight away. Said I was beautiful. But then he turn horrible and control everything I do. He said his mother was ill with cancer... family needed lots of money to help her. But he loved me, and one day he would marry me, and we have children. Live in nice, big house in future. Then my mother and sisters can come to live with us."

Abby shook her head. "Sabina, you're doing really well. You can stop if you need to."

Sabina didn't seem to hear her. She was lost in her own thoughts. There was no expression, no emotion from her, just a matter-of-fact, point-by-point recollection of the events that led her to where she was now – sitting in front of three more strangers, baring her soul.

"I told Johnny I do anything to help him. I love Johnny. He made me think that being with men was only way to raise enough money for mother. One minute he would hug me and say *I love you*; next he shout at me. I wanted to stop, but he said he would kill my mother."

"Where did he take you?" Scott asked.

"A house. Ardit open door; Johnny left me there. He took me into room with small bed. There was a video camera on a stand at end of bed. He... he... just... raped me. He was filming it, and I couldn't move. He smelt bad. Said if I didn't do it, my mother would die..." Her voice trailed off.

Abby placed a hand over her mouth, consumed with a mixture of horror and sadness.

The fucking bastard.

Sabina carried on, not pausing for breath or thought. Her sorrowful story just tumbled out with no end in sight.

"He kept me there. More men came... many each day. They waited outside room. I never stop... ten, twenty, sometimes thirty men every day. One girl in one place... fifty-five men she had sex with before she was sick. He moved me everywhere, hotel room, house, flat."

Scott caught a flicker of fear in her eyes as they flitted from side to side.

"He put knife to throat, said I must earn three to four hundred pounds a day. If not, he would punish me."

"Punish how?"

Sabina shook her head. "No hitting. Didn't want bruises on my body. Raped me all the time. Took me to pub where he showed me basement. There were chains, torn clothes everywhere and tools. Said I would get beaten like other girls and not wake up."

Scott sat up abruptly. "Pub? Did it have a name?"

She paused for a second. "I think... Unicorn."

Scott's heart raced now, the pressure too great. All he wanted to do was close the interview and race to the pub. Every one of his senses was on red alert, his mind racing ahead, but it felt like time had stood still. He couldn't stop. Sabina still had more to say.

"Men pay thirty pounds to have me, but to make more money, he let customers have sex in my behind without condom for sixty pounds." She looked up for the first time, her eyes fixed on to Abby's. "I must see fifteen men a day to pay bills. I owe lots of money to the man who brought me here. Ardit, who take my money, threaten me and say his friends in Albania will hurt my family if I am bad..." Her voice trailed off. Sabina fell silent in the same way she had at the beginning of the interview.

Scott said, "Sabina, you've been very courageous. I'm sorry for what you've been through. I promise we'll bring the men to justice. We will be placing you in protective care for the time being. You're safe now."

Sabina glared at him. "But now my family are not."

34

Abby leant against the wall in the hallway, her hands in her pockets. She was gently tapping her head on the wall, her eyes closed. Scott stood beside her, looking at the floor. They both stood in silence, waiting for their cauldron of emotions to calm down.

Abby opened her eyes and stared up towards the ceiling. "Fuck's sake, guv. You know, in our job we see and hear a lot of shit, and I can handle most things, but that was awful." She let out a long sigh.

Scott placed a reassuring hand on her arm. "You okay?"

She nodded slowly. "Yep, I can't believe one human being could do that to another. We live in such a sick twisted world."

"I know, and it's our job to get justice for that poor girl sitting in there," he replied, flicking his head towards the door. "Let's get the team together for a quick debrief and sort out a plan of action for tomorrow morning."

Scott had pulled in key contacts from the intelligence unit and safeguarding teams to update them on the recent discoveries. The evening sun crept through the briefing room windows, causing those in the direct line of sight to squint. The lack of air conditioning made the room feel stuffy.

Scott started. "Okay, everyone, it's been a challenging day today for many of us, so let's have a round robin and get an update. Abby and I have just interviewed one of the victims, a Sabina Lunga. We found her at the house we raided this afternoon. She's fifteen years old and was trafficked to here from Albania. Sabina's been through a harrowing experience. The interview notes will be in her file for you all to read when you get a moment. She's given us a powerful statement. It's enough for us to bring charges against Ardit Gashi of rape, conspiracy to rape and inciting a child to engage in sexual activity, and that's just for starters. How did you get on with interviewing Gashi, Mike?"

Mike sighed and shook his head. He twisted the corners of his mouth. "Cool as a cucumber, guv. Every question that I or Sian fired at him was met with a *no comment*."

"I'm not surprised, to be honest. From what I've read about Albanian gangs, they operate in small groups bound by a code of silence similar to the Mafia. You've got more chance of squeezing toothpaste out of an empty tube than getting anything out of him. Sabina suggested that Ardit might have a brother who's higher up the command chain. If that is the case, Gashi's hardly going to grass on his own brother. She was brought over by someone we suspect might be Ardit's brother, the one who's controlling this operation. Given that he only comes over here occasionally, he will be harder to track down. And one of the missing girls" – Scott glanced at his notes – "Rishi Mehta, might be in his possession, so it's vital we find her."

The team collectively nodded.

Scott continued, "We found another victim, Kelly Southall, who has been missing from Manchester. Abby, how did you and Raj get on with interviewing her?"

"She's a frightened little girl, guv," Abby replied. "There's a similar pattern emerging here. She was brought down from Manchester by Murat Ahmeti. Kelly was a mess by the time she got here. Murat did exactly what Ardit did to Sabina, but he did it in Manchester." She raised an eyebrow. "Then when she was passed over to Ardit, he did it all over again to stamp his authority and control on her. Oh, and one other thing, Kelly said there are a few other girls. She never got the chance to speak to them, but there's definitely more."

Scott turned to look at the photos of the victims that were pinned to the incident board. He should have felt a sense of relief and elation at having found the missing girls; however, sadness tinged his thoughts. Even though the girls had been indoctrinated into this vile trade long before they appeared on his radar, he wished he had rescued these girls sooner.

Currently, two girls were being whisked away to safety, but they would never be the same again. Their youth had been stolen from them. He couldn't even begin to imagine the psychological damage done.

Scott resumed. "Right, first thing tomorrow, Raj and Sian, I want you to arrest Johnny Wright on suspicion of coercion and grooming underage girls. Bring him back here to interview and grab any computer equipment he has. Sian, I also want you to look at Ardit Gashi's background. Confirm whether he has a brother. Liaise with the intelligence unit on that, and also speak to our colleagues in the Met vice squad. Albanian gangs control at least seventy to eighty per cent of the sex trade in London. Let's see if Ardit or anyone connected to him is known to the teams up in the big smoke."

Scott scribbled a few notes down.

"Mike and Abby, we three will pay Mark Renshaw a visit

tomorrow at the Unicorn pub. Sort out a search warrant for us, please, Abby. Sabina mentioned that Ardit had taken her there as a warning. The suggestion was if she didn't comply, she would be tortured in the basement similar to other girls. Mike, get a couple of uniforms to back us up tomorrow. I'll stop by Matt's desk tonight to forewarn him we might need his SOCO team tomorrow to do a forensic sweep of the basement."

He added. "Raj, you're on late turn tonight, so any new developments, call me."

35

Earlier that day, Scott had popped into the Sainsbury's on Lewes Road to pick up a few bits for dinner. He was hastily preparing his meal when the doorbell rang.

He glanced up at the clock on the wall in his kitchen and noticed that it was exactly eight p.m. He'd had very little time to prepare. Having rushed home from work, Scott had tidied up frantically, showered and changed into a maroon polo T-shirt and pair of jeans.

Upon opening the door, he was lost for words.

Cara stood there in black skintight jeans. She perched elegantly on peep-toe, black platform heels that showed him the smallest hint of red-painted toenails. Her casual blue blouse strained to contain her ample chest; a decorative necklace completed her stunning appearance. Her long brown hair had been straightened and draped elegantly over her shoulders. Scott noticed her red lipstick matched her toenails.

"We can have dinner in the doorway if you want," she suggested, flashing one of her radiant smiles.

"Um... no... shit, you look amazing!" Scott stumbled over his words yet again. "Please come in." He stood to one side and waved her in.

After looking around the lounge, Cara nestled herself into a comfy brown leather sofa whilst Scott went off to fetch two glasses of suitably chilled Pinot Grigio. He came back into the lounge still struggling to stitch a sentence together.

My God, she's so beautiful.

He sat beside her and handed her a glass. They clinked, and each took a sip. Their eyes locked in their own game of *I dare you to turn away first.*

Scott and Cara spent the next few moments recalling how each other's day had gone. There were no false pretences around Cara, no awkward pauses. Scott just felt at ease being in her company. He didn't feel like he was being judged in any way – something he was grateful for given his past.

"Are you hungry?" he asked.

"What for?" she teased, her brightly coloured red lips breaking into a coy smile.

Scott laughed nervously. "For now, food."

It was only when the words fell out of his mouth that he realised he'd said *for now*.

They sat at one end of his dining table. Scott served them warmly baked ciabatta bread slices with a balsamic and Parmesan dipping oil to go along with Mediterranean chicken skewers and wild rice. Scott had put on some chilled R & B music in the lounge, the sounds of which were drifting gently into the dining room.

Cara, clearly hungry, almost polished off two of the three chicken skewers whilst Scott was still on his first.

"How's the food?" he teased.

Cara pointed to her mouth whilst frantically munching. Scott laughed. When Cara tried to speak and ended up choking a little, this made them laugh even more.

She finally composed herself. "This is seriously good. My compliments to the chef," she said, pointing to her plate. "I could get used to this."

"What's your favourite dish?"

She paused for a moment, allowing her eyes to drift up to the ceiling in reflection. "I've not really got a favourite, to be honest – curries, Tex-Mex, Chinese, pub grub..."

"So pretty much anything," he mused.

"Yup, that's me."

Scott treated them to some lemon sorbet before he cleared the table away. It gave Cara an opportunity to wander around his dining room, looking at the various paintings and pictures that he had on the walls. She was staring at some in particular when Scott walked in.

When he saw which ones, Scott stopped in the doorway, unsure what to say.

Cara hesitated. "I'm sorry, I didn't mean to pry... These are some lovely pictures of your wife and daughter."

He joined her and stared fondly at them. "Yes, it's Tina and Becky." His voice cracked a little.

"You must miss them a lot. Becky is the spitting image of her mum."

Scott slowly shook his head, his eyes a little damp. "I do every day. I guess it's why this case is getting to me. When you've been a dad, it changes you. You elevate a whole new level of wanting to protect children, especially your own."

Cara rubbed his arm, understanding the pain he felt.

He didn't have much to say after that, other than to suggest coffee, to which she willingly agreed.

She followed him into the kitchen. As he waited for the kettle to boil, Cara stood beside him and placed one hand on his arm again.

"Scott, I want you to know that I'm here for you. I can't imagine what you've been through, but I care for you. I'm your friend and more if you'll let me be?" She paused. "Losing a child for whatever reason is the hardest thing we will ever experience. We try every day to suppress the sorrow, regret and guilt.

Cara looked deep in thought, leaning against the kitchen counter; a veil of sadness blanketed her face.

"Hey, you okay?" he asked, rubbing her shoulder.

"Yes, I'm fine. I once wanted to have a family too, but it didn't work out..." she said.

Scott turned to her properly. Her dark brown eyes offered him sensitivity, compassion and desire. "I know you care, and I can't thank you enough."

"I'm not here to hurt you, Scott. I want to be here for you if you're willing to let me in."

They stood closer, not deliberately, more an unconscious force drawing them towards one another.

Scott moved to stand in front of her, their bodies just a few inches apart. They both felt that strong pull of magnetic attraction, that intangible bond that happens between two people attracted to each other. It was energetic. It was raw. It was sexual. But it was more than that... it was a desire to know each other intimately. Really know each other.

In the silent space they shared, Scott could hear her breathe; her eyes remained firmly fixed on his.

"I like you, Cara... I really like you."

"The feeling is mutual," she said softly.

He leant in and gave her a delicate kiss on the cheek, then wrapped his arms around her waist.

She responded by leaning in and turning her face to meet his lips. Seconds later, they locked in a deep, passionate kiss, his tongue searching her mouth. They were still hungry, but for each other this time.

Cara cupped his head, pulling his mouth closer to her, silently asking him to explore her further.

Scott had finally let down his guard. Perhaps now was the time for him to accept things and move on.

They only had one thing on their minds as Scott took her by the hand and led her upstairs.

36

A buzzing noise sounded close to Scott's right ear.

His senses tried to comprehend what had woken him from his deep, blissful sleep. The buzzing continued. He opened one eye, still adjusting to the brightness flooding into the room. It was only then he realised it was his phone alerting him to a text message.

He stared at the digital screen, his eyes fighting to focus through the tiny slits he'd made. Upon opening the message, he saw it was a text message from Raj. His eyes widened, and his senses fired into action as he took in every word.

Press appeal for Christine Newland has drawn a positive sighting. A computer shop owner recalls her coming in to drop off a laptop. The computer shop found messages of an inappropriate nature. Christine was informed. She came in and collected the laptop immediately.

Scott fired back a message as quickly as his fingers would allow him. Then he lay on his back, thinking about Raj's message. The events of last night came to him. He turned over to see Cara still fast asleep.

Her long brown hair framed her beautiful face. He reflected on the night they'd shared. Their steamy, passionate encounter. He marvelled at the sensuality she exuded, her lack of inhibition and her insatiable sexual appetite. He had enjoyed every moment of slowly undressing her. When he'd finally pressed his firm body against her soft skin, it felt like the Fourth of July inside him, every cell of his body exploding.

The room felt stuffy now. A hot sex smell and a humid night filled the room. A thin bed sheet partially covered Cara, one breast exposed. Scott bent forward and kissed it. Her skin felt soft, just as he remembered it from last night.

He left a note on his pillow, telling her he'd been called out early on police business and that he would speak to her later. He signed off with a suggestion to help herself to a shower and breakfast, followed by two kisses.

Scott found the computer shop tucked away in Bath Street, close to the station – a small, white-fronted shop squashed between a café and a second-hand furniture shop that had a variety of tables, chairs, cupboards and wooden doors outside. The old luggage trunks grabbed Scott's interest in particular. They looked out of place sitting on the pavement outside the shop. He thought they would have been better suited in the lounge of a large, period-style house.

The computer shop itself was long and narrow; Scott estimated it to be no wider than eight feet from wall to wall. The sign above the door said *Ctrl R for Repair*, which made Scott smile.

Nice name.

As he entered, he was hit by an oppressive heat. It was warming up outside, but the addition of several laptops and computers all running and kicking out heat caused Scott to loosen his tie. A tall man of Afro-Caribbean descent, with thick black-rimmed glasses and sporting a large stomach that hung over the front of his jeans, was busily peering inside the casing of a PC tower. He prodded the innards with an exceptionally long screwdriver.

"Jori Grant?" Scott shouted, causing the man to jump.

He peered up, looking over the top rim of his glasses. "Yes, that's me. Can I help you?"

Scott showed him his warrant card. "I'm Detective Scott Baker from Brighton CID. I understand you spoke to one of my colleagues about Christine Newland?"

The man nodded. He rose from his seat to meet Scott at the counter. "Yes, I did. Not sure what else I can tell you."

"I'm leading the investigation into her murder, and we're trying to build a picture of her last movements. I understand she came in and dropped off a laptop. Can you tell me what happened?"

Jori Grant adjusted his glasses, pushing them towards the bridge of his nose. "Yes, she dropped off a laptop on the seventh, and later that morning, I got round to inspecting it. She said it was her daughter's laptop and that she'd complained about it crashing all the time. She was getting a blue screen."

Scott wasn't sure what a blue screen was. He'd never been that technically minded, but guessed it wasn't normal if it needed to be taken in.

"I went through it but noticed in her browsing history lots of chat history from a chat room that her daughter must have been on. And to be honest, it wasn't a pleasant conversation. It was quite explicit with whoever she was chatting with." Jori shifted uncomfortably, not looking entirely happy about what he'd found. "Then, stored in the downloads folder were quite a few pictures of a bloke's cock. In a pictures folder there were a few pictures of a young girl who'd taken selfies..." Grant shrugged. "You know that type of stuff."

Scott shook his head. "No, I don't. What do you mean?"

Grant hesitated for a moment. "Um... Well, they were topless shots she'd taken in the mirror."

"What happened next?"

"Well, the first thing I do whenever I get a piece of hardware that's got something of a sexual nature on it is to contact the person who brought it in. I contacted Christine Newland within a few hours of her dropping it off. She seemed horrified. She said that she'd be back to pick it up and that she would deal with it."

"And did she come in?"

"Yes. She came in about one thirty p.m. the same day. She looked concerned, and that was *before* I showed her the content. I went through it with her, and the colour drained from her face. She grabbed the laptop and left in quite a hurry. Mrs Newland said she'd get back to me. Next thing I know, I see her picture in *The Argus* that she'd been murdered. That's when I called in."

Scott could gauge the man's concern and shock that a customer of his had been murdered by the worry lines on his forehead.

"Okay, thank you, Mr Grant. You've been helpful. I'll arrange for one of my officers to pop down later to get a proper witness statement recorded."

"Sure, anything. It's a tragedy," he said, shaking his head slowly. He turned to carry on working on the PC tower.

As Scott walked back to the car, he called Abby. The moment she picked up, he filled her in on what he'd discovered about the laptop and Christine Newland.

His next stop would be the Newlands'.

37

Alan and Lucy Newland were at home, as Scott expected. They were no doubt still reeling from the death of Christine. As he pulled up outside, there was still a steady stream of visitors coming and going from the house, probably paying their respects and rallying round the pair.

Scott was about to ring the doorbell when the door opened. A middle-aged woman stepped out of the house, tissue in hand, dabbing her eyes and sniffing. He moved to one side to let her pass before entering.

Alan and Lucy were sitting in the lounge; Alan had a protective arm around his daughter, who was softly sobbing into his chest. He looked up to see Scott entering the room, his eyes widening, no doubt hoping for some news – and answers.

Alan looked a broken man. His stubble from the other night was now the beginnings of a beard. His eyes looked tired and sore; his face had aged considerably with worry, sadness and confusion etched all over it. Lucy was curled up into her dad's chest, her eyes pinched tight, tears leaking out the corners and down her cheeks.

"Have you got any news?" Alan Newland asked, staring hopefully into Scott's eyes. He was desperate for answers, any answers, anything that would help explain why Christine had been killed.

"Our investigation is still ongoing, and I'm afraid it's still early days. We've had a fairly good response to our press appeal, which is why I'm here today."

Alan Newland paid more attention, homing in on what Scott was saying.

"We have a bit of a delicate situation here, and unfortunately there's never a good time to talk about this. Following the press appeal, we received information about a sighting of your wife on the day she disappeared. She apparently took in Lucy's laptop to an internet shop because I understand it was crashing all the time." He looked at the daughter. "Is that correct?"

Alan checked with Lucy, and through the tears, she nodded slowly.

Scott cleared his throat. "When the laptop was examined, inappropriate content was found on it. Christine was informed about it. She went back in and collected the laptop around one thirty p.m. on the day that she went missing."

Alan looked confused. "Inappropriate content?"

Scott shifted his attention between Alan and Lucy. He noticed that Lucy was now staring at him, her eyes wide, her pupils dilated – with surprise or fear, he wasn't sure.

Scott continued, "There were images of a man's genitals in the downloads folder and images of a topless girl too. There was also a detailed chat history between whoever was using the laptop and another person." Focusing his attention on Lucy, he said, "I believe this is your laptop, Lucy. Would you know anything about this?"

Alan turned to look at his daughter again, confusion contorting his face. "Lucy?"

She had the look of a scared little girl, unable to explain, paralysed by fear. Her eyes darted between her father and Scott, not knowing whom to address or what to say.

"Lucy, were you having an online chat conversation with someone of the opposite sex? Were photos exchanged between you?" Scott asked gently, leaning his elbows on his knees and cupping his hands together.

Lucy squirmed. He couldn't tell if it was with guilt or embarrassment. The fact that this matter was being discussed in front of her father was probably making the conversation even more uncomfortable.

Her legs were pulled up into her chest; her hands were tightly interlocked around her shins. She bit on her bottom lip, looked away, and then nodded once.

"Lucy, what was his name?" Scott asked.

A long pause followed. Still staring at one corner of the room, she whispered, "Johnny."

Scott became more alert. "Lucy, listen carefully. What were the last things you discussed?"

Hesitantly, she replied, "We arranged to meet at Hove Park the evening Mum went missing." She sobbed loudly and stared at Scott. "It's my fault, my fault she died, isn't it?"

Alan's protective hand had fallen loose from her; he was clearly numbed by what he was hearing.

Scott continued, "Lucy, I need you to get the laptop for me. We need to examine it. Could you please get it for me now?"

Lucy unfurled her legs and stood up. She glanced at her dad. "I'm so sorry."

When the girl left, Alan asked Scott, "Do you think this thing on the computer and my wife's death are connected?"

"Unfortunately I'm not at liberty to speculate. We need to

examine the laptop first to look for any evidence or clues that might help us to understand the last few hours of your wife's life. As soon as I know more, I will let you know."

Scott was certain the two were connected, and now he had a name: Johnny.

38

Back at the station, Scott made arrangements for Lucy's laptop to be taken to the high-tech unit for analysis as a priority case. On the phone, he stressed to the forensic computer examiner the urgency of extracting vital evidence that could determine the potential killer in an ongoing investigation. He instructed the examiner to cross-reference data with a Dell laptop seized from Johnny Wright.

The examiner was less than cooperative, citing a huge backlog in examining mobile phones and computers. He ended the call making no promises, much to Scott's frustration.

A quick chat with DCI Harvey would help to push things along.

Scott could sense it. Today would be a busy but crucial day.

He grabbed Abby and Mike, and the three made their way to the Unicorn pub. As he drove, he filled them in on his visit to the computer shop that morning and the subsequent discovery of an online discussion between Lucy and someone who went by the name of Johnny.

Scott pulled the car up outside the Unicorn, where they were met by two uniformed officers who were waiting outside, sipping on coffee from white Styrofoam cups. The pub was currently closed. Opening time was twelve noon, which would give Scott and his team ample opportunity to search the establishment.

He banged on the door several times with a clenched fist. He waited a few moments, exchanging glances with the other officers.

Not wishing to lose his man, Scott instructed one uniformed officer to check the side and back to make sure that no one was making a break for it. Scott banged again several times, this time harder, causing the door to rattle.

From somewhere within the pub, someone was shouting, "I'm coming... What's the hurry?"

A series of clunks indicated that several bolts were being unlocked. The door finally opened.

Mark Renshaw stood there rubbing his eyes, clearly woken up by the disturbance, his eyes crusty and narrowed as the bright sunlight caught him off guard. The sight of four police officers standing on his doorstep agitated Renshaw. His eyes darted from one officer to another.

"What do you want now?" he groaned, his throat sounding dry and parched.

"Good morning, Mr Renshaw," Scott said with a sarcastic smile. "We would like to come in and have a chat, if that's okay."

"Listen, I don't know what this is about, but I've told you everything I know. I'm a busy man. The pub's opening shortly," he said through gritted teeth. He was clearly frustrated and annoyed by this intrusion, barely able to restrain his anger.

Scott didn't ask again. He pushed past Renshaw; the other officers followed. "New evidence has come to light from a credible witness that suggests girls have been sexually abused and tortured in your basement. We have a warrant to have a look," he said, pulling the document from inside his jacket, his eyes firmly fixed on Renshaw.

Renshaw swallowed nervously and licked his lips, frozen to the spot and unable to respond. He nervously looked around the pub.

"You can't just barge in here!" he fumed, trying to buy himself time.

Scott noticed Mike's agitation with Renshaw's delaying tactics, as Mike's eyes narrowed and his forehead twitched.

Scott said, "Well, Mr Renshaw, you're implicated in the rape and torture of girls on your property. You're also implicated in having sex with an underage girl who died within hours of seeing you. We also have you on a charge of supplying drugs to an underage girl who died within hours of seeing you. You're in a big pile of elephant shit up to your neck. As far as I can see, you've just traded your last day."

Renshaw's brow was sweating; he ran his hands through his hair, nervously pacing back and forth, staring wildly at the floor. The two uniformed officers moved into position behind Renshaw, just in case there was a change in his behaviour and he needed to be restrained.

Renshaw's character morphed in front of them. He became a gibbering wreck, muttering to himself. "They made me... they made me... they forced me... I can't stop them; they'll kill me."

"I want you to stay here with the two uniformed officers, Mr Renshaw, whilst we go down to have a look," Scott said in a firm, directive tone.

Renshaw didn't acknowledge Scott, his hands gripping his head, too consumed by his own deep thoughts.

Scott led Mike and Abby down a series of worn concrete steps into the dark and dingy cellar. He tapped the wall with one hand, searching for the light, whilst he steadied himself with his other hand on the wall. Finally finding the switch, he flicked it on. A single bulb cast a dull glow around the basement as they reached the bottom step.

The cellar was a cold, dark and damp place. The only sounds around them were their own footsteps and breathing.

It took a moment for Scott's eyes to adjust to the semi-darkness. The room had a lowered ceiling, which left little headroom, forcing Scott to bend his neck. He saw a long room ahead of them, with bare brick walls that had been organised into two sections.

Immediately in front of them were several rows of beer kegs. One line of kegs was positioned against the wall, attached to plastic lines that disappeared into the roof cavity and likely ended up behind the bar. But it was the space beyond the kegs that alerted Scott.

The three of them walked a few feet before stopping. A partition wall with a door had been built across the far end of the cellar. Scott reached for the handle. He pushed the door open, but stopped, shocked by what he saw. He stretched out both arms to stop Abby and Mike from moving any farther into the room. They stood in silence, taking in how this section of the room had been remodelled.

"Christ," was all that Abby could muster.

On the wall to the left were two thick chains anchored into the wall, about six feet from the floor. At the end of each chain was a handcuff. To the right of them and up against the wall lay a beer keg on its side. Attached to the wall above it were two hooks, each with a pair of handcuffs hanging from them.

Scott stared in disbelief, unable to comprehend what atrocities had taken place here, and what the victims had suffered. His attention was drawn away when Abby nudged him in the ribs. He looked to where she was staring.

On the floor close by lay a small, light blue T-shirt, with dark brown splatters. Not far from it was a hammer, a screwdriver and several pairs of pliers of different shapes and sizes. Empty bottles of Holsten Pils were scattered around them. Based on the conversation with Sabina, it was likely that this was where the girls had been plied with drink before being tortured and raped.

His gut churned.

"Mike, go upstairs and arrest that shit. Abby, can you get on to scientific services? We need SOCO to do a full sweep here."

He surveyed the scene, haunted by the words Sabina had uttered in her interview. A cold shiver ran down his spine. He wasn't sure if it was due to the temperature of the cellar or the emotions that washed over him from his guilt and regret for not helping these girls sooner.

39

Mark Renshaw sat in the interview suite accompanied by his solicitor, a short, squat dumpy man Scott recognised as a duty solicitor with whom he'd frequently clashed horns. He was a man who relished the opportunity to scrutinise and dissect any case that his clients found themselves in.

Renshaw looked terrified and jittery. Scott and Abby joined them in the room. Abby did the formal introductions, reasons for arrest and activation of the voice recorder.

Renshaw had been advised by his solicitor to offer nothing more than *no comment* to the questions posed by the officers. Simple questions like how long he'd run the pub? Who else had access to the basement? And how much was he aware of in terms of what was going on down there?

They were all met with the proverbial, but shaky "no comment."

Scott continued, unperturbed. He needed to push Renshaw, get this man talking. In Scott's favour, he had a very detailed witness statement from Sabina, but to continue building a tight case, he needed Renshaw onside.

If there was one weak link in the trafficking operation, it was this man.

"Did you know girls were being tortured in your basement?" Scott asked.

"No comment."

"Did you take part in the systematic torture and rape of girls in your cellar?"

"No comment."

Scott decided to change tactics. Renshaw was as closed as a clamshell, and he needed to steam this guy open.

"Did you hear Libby Stevens cry and plead for her life when you tortured her there?" he asked, hands flat on the table, leaning in to Renshaw.

That statement sparked visible pain that contorted and twisted Renshaw's face. Saliva dribbled from his mouth. He had his eyelids closed tight, trying to hold back the tide of tears that threatened to escape.

Scott pushed Renshaw even harder. He needed to – he wanted to break the man.

"You said, 'They made me... they forced me... I can't stop them; they'll kill me'... Who forced you, Renshaw? Who can't you stop? Who will kill you? I need names, and I need them now!" Scott slammed his fist on the table, causing Renshaw and his ruddy-faced solicitor to jump.

Renshaw's solicitor burst into life. "May I remind you, Detective Inspector, that my client is not at liberty to answer any of your questions, nor do I advocate your treatment and style of questioning either," he replied, poker-faced.

Scott glared at the solicitor, enjoying the gladiatorial battle that was now taking shape. He had them both rattled.

"I'm sorry, I'm sorry, I didn't realise it would go this far," Renshaw pleaded.

"What went too far, Renshaw? You raping young girls?

You getting your kicks from humiliating young, vulnerable girls?" Scott pushed.

"No... no... it wasn't me. What *they* did with the girls."

Renshaw's solicitor was furiously remonstrating now, advising Renshaw to say nothing more.

"Who are we talking about?" Scott pushed. "Come on, Renshaw, you're doing well; you've come this far; you might as well get it off your chest. Do the right thing for the first time in your life!"

Renshaw shook his head. "They'll kill me. I can't say."

"Well, you have two choices. You can help us to catch the people who committed these vile crimes – the judge will be more lenient with you because you helped us with our enquiries. Or you can continue to protect those people, who will continue to make your life a misery whether that be *inside* or outside prison."

Renshaw sighed in desperation as he saw his world falling apart around him. "It was Ardit Gashi and his henchmen. They were bringing girls in the pub to ply them with drink, get them drunk, doing stuff to them before moving them on elsewhere. It was the process."

"What part did you play in it?" Abby asked.

Renshaw hesitated for a moment, clearly trying to find the right way to structure his reply. "In return for using my pub and my booze, they let me have a go with the girls."

"What do you mean, 'Have a go with the girls'?" Scott probed.

Renshaw shrugged. "Well, by the time they were drunk, they were just lying on the floor like a sack of shit, so they let me do whatever I wanted to them. It was a free shag."

"And what happened to Libby Stevens?"

Renshaw folded again, wringing his hands together, riddled with guilt. He cried out, his voice broken, like the rest of him, "She was different, she'd been to the pub a long time ago, but he brought her back. She was crying and screaming, so Ardit and a few others beat her up. They went too far..." His voice trailed off.

"What happened next?" Scott asked.

"I begged them to stop. I didn't want any more to do with this. I told them to look for somewhere else, but they wouldn't take no for an answer. That's when they came back and smashed up the place and beat me up."

"To silence you?" Scott asked.

Renshaw nodded, his guilt exposed, his downfall complete.

40

A rank-tasting coffee from the drinks machine and a few packets of Bourbon biscuits would suffice for a late lunch. Scott hurried from the interview, keen to update the DCI.

DCI Harvey was sitting in her office, humming to herself as usual. His knock on the door interrupted what pleasant thoughts she was no doubt entertaining.

She looked up to see Scott and waved him in. "I had the superintendent on the phone earlier this morning asking for an update. So damn handy you turned up. What have you got for me?"

"Things are shaping up nicely, ma'am. We've just arrested the landlord of the Unicorn pub following interviews with the two victims we extracted from the house. Renshaw was allowing one of the suspects to use his pub for the torture and rape of girls. I've got forensics combing over it at the moment. There's plenty of evidence I'm confident will confirm it."

"Good, good," she replied.

"Ardit Gashi, whom we arrested at the house, is failing to

cooperate. To be honest, there's plenty of evidence to implicate him with or without his statement. One of the victims has positively ID'd him from photos. The punter that uniform picked up after he left the house admitted paying thirty pounds for sex with one of the victims. Cash has been exchanged in return for sex. I think it's moving in the right direction. One of the suspects in the frame, Johnny Wright, is now complicit in the coercion and grooming of girls. Some of the team picked him up this morning. The rest I can update you on later?"

"Jolly good, Scott. Give me a shout if you need my help," the DCI replied. Her smug grin grew wider, making it clear she wasn't going to get another ass kicking from the superintendent.

As he left the DCI's office, his phone vibrated in his pocket. Reaching for it, he saw it was a text from Cara.

> *Hey handsome, did my breath smell that much that you had to leave first thing in the morning? LOL... Only joking! Missed you this morning, had a nice relaxing shower before heading off to work. Wish you could have joined me!!! Had a really nice time last night. Hope there's no regrets?? C xx*

Reading the text brought a smile to Scott's face. His mind drifted back to last night, less than twelve hours ago, which seemed a distant memory with all he'd been through so far today. For the first time in as long as he could remember, he felt excited about his life. He'd worried so much about betraying Tina's trust and memory. But she was probably up there wagging her finger at him, telling him to get on with his life.

He typed out a reply.

Your breath did honk!!... Only joking. Had a lovely time last night. Wish I could have been there to see you wake up. Look forward to the next time you fancy a shower. X

He hit send and focused on the task in hand.

Scott raced back to his desk and fired up his PC. He had a long list of emails still needing his attention. At the last count, he had a running total of two hundred and twenty-five to work through. Most were internal memos or emails about news articles on policing or Google alerts. He knew today he'd only be able to clear a dozen or so emails.

He shouted from his desk, beckoning Sian in.

Sian marched in, a notepad under her arm. "Yes, guv?"

"How did you get on with looking into Gashi's background?"

"I've got some promising information, guv. Ardit has a brother called Korab Gashi; he's known to run trafficking, sex and prostitution rings in Albania and over here in the UK. He's been tracked a few times entering the country by our colleagues in the Met vice unit. He only comes over once or twice a year. Their officers find it hard to track him because he uses different ports each time – Dover, Newhaven, Folkestone, Harwich, you name it. He's got convictions back in Albania for human trafficking and prostitution. The Met boys have broken up a couple of his operations in London, but no sooner has one operation shut down than another opens up. Plenty of foot soldiers at his disposal. And he's nowhere in sight."

Scott mulled over the intelligence. "The chances of catching him are small, but my guess is he's still in the country, because we still haven't been able to locate Rishi Mehta. We need to find her before she disappears for good." He nodded. "At least we can now assume that his brother Ardit is running one of the operations for him in the UK."

Sian continued, "We've got Johnny in a holding cell. The funny thing is, guv, he does not seem to be the slightest bit worried that we're charging him with the coercion and grooming of underage girls. He just doesn't seem to be bothered. He keeps saying that he'll be out soon."

"Well, to be honest, Sian, he came across as a smooth character when I first met him. We have a powerful victim statement, so he's not going anywhere in a hurry. Okay, good job, Sian, keep me informed." Scott checked the email in his inbox from the high-tech unit. He knew the DCI would come in handy. "Looks like I'm popping along to forensics. They're pulling off some history on the laptop I recovered this morning."

41

Tim Coburn was the forensic computer examiner Scott had spoken to earlier that morning. As he stopped by his desk, Coburn was on his phone, having a personal conversation judging by what Scott overheard.

"Yes, love, I promise I will be home by six tonight... yes... yes... I know... yes, and I know it's my turn to take Chloe for her swimming lesson..."

He shot Scott an embarrassed glance as he endeavoured to stop his wife from continuing to give him a hard time. "Got to go, love. Someone wants to speak to me. Love you lots."

Scott stood there with folded arms. He wasn't opposed to people having personal conversations at work, but it did rile him when the conversations were loud enough for everyone in earshot to have a ringside seat.

"I got your email, Tom. What have you got for me?" he asked, messing up his name on purpose.

He looked around the workstation. There were clear evidence bags scattered around containing mobile phones of all shapes and sizes. The large workbench behind Tim had larger, clear plastic evidence bags containing laptops and PC towers. Scott estimated there must have been at least a dozen or so such bags. The DCI's intervention had fast-tracked his request to the top of the list, much to his relief.

"And it's Tim, actually," the examiner replied, annoyed.

Scott suppressed a laugh.

Serves you right for keeping me waiting.

"And?" Scott said, circling his hand, suggesting that Tim get on with it.

"I had a look at that computer you left this morning. Still needs more work, but I found a chat history. Here, have a look at this printout." Tim thrust a sheet of computer paper towards Scott.

Scott glanced at it and scanned through a section of the conversation.

Lucy: I'm Lucy Newland btw, nice to meet you (smiley face symbol).

Johnny: Johnny here. Pleased to meet you too, Lucy.

Lucy: Thank you.

Johnny: You are cute btw.

Lucy: Well, I wouldn't go that far but thanks.

Johnny: I love your eyes in your profile pic.

Lucy: They're my mum's eyes LOL.

Johnny: I can't stop looking at it.

Lucy: She has the same eyes.

Johnny: Is she as pretty as you though?

Lucy: Yes she's a beautiful woman.

Johnny: Random question for you... what's yr bra size?

Lucy: That was a bit random.

Johnny: I did say it was a random question. Not going to answer it...?

Lucy: Do you always ask random questions, Johnny? I'm a B cup.

Johnny: Oh that's a nice handful. He he. (smiley face emoji).

Lucy: Cheeky.

Johnny: Have any boys been lucky enough to see them or even get to play with them?

Lucy: Most boys at my school are idiots. CBA. So no, none of them.

Johnny: Never taken a pic of them?

Lucy: Never really had a reason to.

Johnny: Bet they look amazing like you.

Lucy: LOL. I see them every day.

Johnny: Lucky you. I wish I could see! [devil face emoji].

Lucy: I'm not sure, my dad will kill me if he found out cus I'm only 14?

Johnny: How wud he find out?

Johnny: U don't tell him, it's just fun

Johnny: We r not having sex

Johnny: Just seeing

Lucy: I know but I'm still a child and ur an adult, is that ok?

Scott had read enough.

"That's quite a telling conversation," he said, reading that short extract again. "Any feedback on the IP address Johnny was using?"

Tim shook his head. "I'm afraid not, I'm still looking into it, but from what I can see, multiple IP addresses are being used."

"Meaning?"

"Well, it's quite possible that Johnny was tapping into Wi-Fi hotspots, so he wasn't static in one place. Each and every time you log into a laptop or PC, your internet service provider gives you a one-off IP address, which they call a dynamic IP address."

"Any facials stored on the computer?"

With a shrug Tim said, "No. A few pictures of male genitals, female breasts, and harmless pictures of lots of teens hanging out together in and out of school. Most are mobile phone downloads but nothing else. If you were hoping for a facial shot, your man was too clever."

"Anything on the second laptop that corresponds with the first?"

"Sorry, there's nothing on there at all in relation to online chat histories, images, emails –nothing. It's as clean as a whistle. It's got the usual stuff on there like web page history of sites like Pornhub, but the pages he visited were not teen related. It was stuff that most men look at."

That wasn't what Scott wanted to hear. He desperately needed to prove that the Johnny in this online conversation was the same Johnny they had in the custody suite downstairs.

"Okay, keep me posted if you extract more information."

With that, Tim turned back to his workstation and busily scanned through a page of what looked like numbers to Scott. No doubt they meant something far more interesting to those more IT savvy than him.

42

Scott sat at his desk, sipping more cups of stale coffee as the evening wore on. He couldn't understand why he kept drinking the station's machine coffee that tasted no better than pond water in his opinion.

The first signs of a headache were fast looming. Despite his coffee consumption, his mouth felt dry and dehydrated. He had been on the go all day and hadn't drunk any water. He'd need fluids soon if he wanted to grab a quick run on the seafront later.

Right now, the cases needed his attention. They were bothering him for multiple reasons. Scott hated loose ends; his job was to gather evidence and tie up those loose ends. But it was the legwork in between that frustrated him more than anything else.

On a notepad, he'd sketched out the case: the names of the girls, the names of those arrested, and had drawn connections between them all. There were still a few pieces of the jigsaw missing. He was sure this team had taken out a few key players in the ring, but the ringleader, Korab Gashi, was unaccounted for.

More importantly, Rishi Mehta, another victim, was still out there somewhere, and who knew what condition she was in. Had she endured the same fate as Sabina or Kelly? What stage of the *process* was she at? Would they be too late? Was it now a matter of finding her body?

Scott stared blankly at his screen and accepted the possibility that Rishi wasn't the only one still unaccounted for. The sad fact was he was no closer to finding them. He needed to lean on those he already had in custody. He was certain that Renshaw knew nothing more. Gashi wasn't about to squeal on his brother. Intelligence from other cities had offered no new information.

Now there was a new string to his investigation: Lucy and Christine Newland.

Had Johnny Wright been grooming Lucy, or was the chat name Johnny a coincidence? Did Johnny kill Christine?

They had another weak link in the trafficking chain – Johnny Wright. The lowlife would be his next port of call.

Scott was just about to head back into the interview suite to grill Johnny again when Raj raced along the corridor towards him. Today had been a long day.

Scott leant against the wall outside the suite, the incessant last few days beginning to take their toll. But his adrenaline spurring him to find Rishi kept tiredness at bay.

"What's up, Raj?"

"Just had a call from uniform, guv. They stopped a blue Fiat Ducato van on a routine pull for a broken tail light, which turned out to have defective tyres too."

"That's a traffic offence. What's that to do with us?"

"It's not the van that's of interest to us, guv, it's what they found inside that is, and who was driving it."

Scott shot him a curious look.

"It's Robert Shaw. Uniform smelt cannabis on him and

inside the cab of the van, so they searched it. Officers called us in when they found a bloodied chair leg in the back, and what appears to be bloodstained towels and blankets."

"Human blood?"

"Don't know, guv. The van's been impounded, and they're awaiting other officers to arrive. The van and driver are being brought here."

"Okay, keep me posted, Raj. I'm about to have a quick chat with our man Johnny, but put SOCO on standby, and have a look over the contents when the van arrives here."

With that, Raj was off again, clearly excited at getting stuck into some action rather than being the officer tasked with manning the phones.

Scott entered the suite. Although Johnny Wright had been stuck in a small cell alone, giving him time to contemplate the charges brought against him, the man appeared unaffected. He maintained his unfaltering cool, calm exterior as he sat opposite Scott. A duty solicitor was the only other person present.

Scott took a moment to observe Wright. He was leaning back in his chair, his arms hanging by his sides, nonchalantly slouched low, as so many of his generation would do in normal circumstances. He was either a superb actor or just plain stupid.

"Johnny, we need your help," Scott started. "We've got at least one girl missing, and we need to find her. Do you have any idea where Ardit could be keeping her or any other girls?"

A derisive smile broke out on Johnny's face as he sat up in his chair. Locking both hands and resting them on the table, he paused, looked up at the ceiling and then replied, "Now why would I want to help the filth?"

"Because there's a young girl missing. She has a family, a

mother and father who want her back." Scott knew that probably wasn't the case, but he needed any angle to get the information he needed.

A slow sarcastic shake of the head was the only response Wright gave.

"Johnny, there's nothing left now. Everyone in the ring is under arrest. Renshaw is in another room singing his heart out. He's dropping you all in it. There is no loyalty; it's every man for himself. He knows that helping us now could work in his favour, ensuring a lighter sentence in the long run." Scott let that hang in the air and twiddled a pen around his fingers.

Johnny shrugged, the silence in the room battling the day-to-day noise of station banter and footsteps in the corridor that permeated the room.

Scott said, "Jenna loves you, you do know that?"

The change in topic caused a flicker in Johnny's eyes. Scott could see it. She was just another pawn in a game, a vile business, but the flicker hinted that perhaps Jenna was different. Did he like her, or was she unfinished business?

"Give her some closure, Johnny. Let her get on with her life."

"Oh, don't worry, she'll get closure all right, sooner than she thinks," Johnny fired back, his face animated for the first time during this interview.

"What does that mean? Is she in danger? If she means anything to you, now's the time to man up."

As if realising the fruitlessness of his defence, Johnny looked down at the table, in deep thought, possibly having an internal duel. It might be finally dawning on him: he was trapped between the devil and the deep blue sea.

Johnny's shoulders drooped. "Listen, all I know is that they used to keep the girls at an address in Twyford Road, and exchanges took place in Freshfield Way. The next swap is within the next two days. That is all I know. The less I know, the better."

Scott breathed a sigh of relief. "You did the right thing."

43

Twyford Road was situated on the northernmost edge of Brighton, close to the Stanmer Halls of Residence that were part of the University of Brighton. From the outside, the inconspicuous address offered no hint to its real identity as a holding house for girls trafficked and forced into prostitution. A generic semi-detached house blended into the background, giving no reason for the neighbours to be concerned.

Scott knew the area well, having stayed at the Varley Halls of Residence whilst studying at the university. The halls weren't far from the location they were heading to.

Scott and Abby, together with the tactical entry team, drove to the house at speed, screeching to a halt in the evening darkness. Ten pairs of boots bailed out, thundering along the pavement to the location.

The door offered little resistance to the mighty "red enforcer" being carried by a burly uniformed officer. The officer quickly moved to one side to allow the remaining officers entry.

They raced in shouting, "Police! Stay where you are!" A

cacophony of sounds echoed through the house and out on to the street, alerting the neighbours. They came outside, curiosity getting the better of them.

The officers raced from one room to the next, illumination from their large torch lights casting ghoulish shadows that bounced off the walls. But it soon became clear to Scott that they were too late.

The property was unfurnished apart from one front room that had four makeshift mattresses haphazardly arranged on the floor, covered with loose and dirty bed coverings. Temporary floral curtains hung from the wall, shielding the outside world, and empty Pot Noodle cartons were strewn on the kitchen floor.

"They lived in pretty basic conditions, guv," Abby said as she joined him.

Anger caught hold. He grunted, "Hmm."

"The kettle is still warm, so someone was here recently."

44

Scott cleared his head with an early morning run along the seafront. The sun was still hiding behind thin, wispy cirrus cloud, and there was coolness in the air. As he made his way back from Palace Pier, the low hum of busy commuter traffic along the Kingsway was drowned out by the music pumping through his headphones. The demands of the job and irregular hours took precedence, making it increasingly difficult to switch off and enjoy the downtime. He relished these moments.

With a cool breeze on his face and the repetitive beat of his pounding feet reverberating through his body, the tension drained from every pore.

He'd grabbed a couple of chicken shish takeaways last night after Cara had called him late, asking if he fancied company – an offer he happily accepted. Despite the lateness, they'd enjoyed their meal. The mood had been tinged with slight coyness after their night together. But they soon got over their shyness. Their hunger for each other had led to passionate lovemaking right there on the dining table before they'd both collapsed into bed and fallen asleep in each other's arms.

A smile broke on his face as he recalled the uninhibited and spontaneous moment between them. The fact that they'd had little opportunity to undress made the moment even more intense. He felt alive for the first time in a long time, and excited now at the prospect of seeing more of her.

Scott's moment of joy was interrupted by an incoming call. He slowed his pace to a gentle jog and glanced at the screen belted to his bicep. It was Abby.

Stopping by the side and perching one heel on the promenade railings to stretch his hamstring, he answered.

"Can't you survive one morning without me?" he teased.

"In your dreams," she said before her tone changed. "It's Jenna Wade... she was abducted this morning. Leaving Benedict's on her way to school, she was bundled into a car."

"Pick me up from mine in fifteen minutes," he replied with urgency.

As Abby pulled up to the residential unit, Scott wished he had driven. His DS had skipped vital parts of the Highway Code to get them there fast.

"Remind me to drive next time," he insisted, getting out of the car.

Abby cast him one of her disparaging looks as she did the same. "You have as much road sense as a blindfolded tortoise. A passenger in your car needs to take out extra life insurance."

She walked ahead of him.

"Less of that, Sergeant," he called after her. "Don't forget I'm still your boss."

Scott hated being criticised for his driving. Even though it was harmless banter between them, Abby loved winding him up.

They found Jean Temple, the residential unit manager, in the back of an ambulance, being tended to for a minor head injury.

Scott rested one foot on the footplate for the rear of the ambulance. "Are you okay, Mrs Temple?"

"Yes, I'll live," she replied a little shakily.

"What happened?"

"When I last looked, Jenna was outside having a cigarette. I was in the office. I heard some shouting and a few screams. By the time I ran outside, she was already being bundled into a car by two men. I tried to intervene, but one of the guys punched me and pushed me to the floor. I tried to stop them, but the driver just sped off and caught me with the wing mirror."

"Any idea on the car?" Abby asked, making notes.

Jean Temple grimaced as a sharp pain shot through her side. "It was a dark Audi, that's all I can remember. It happened so quickly."

Scott nodded in sympathy. "What did the men look like?"

Jean paused for a moment, trying hard to stir her memory into action. "They were darker in appearance, certainly not English by the way they were shouting. More foreign sounding."

Scott and Abby exchanged a glance.

"Okay, that's helpful," Scott said. "Anything else?"

"Jenna was screaming, trying to resist, but they dragged her into the car. She asked them where they were taking her."

"And what did they say?"

Jean looked up at Scott, tears in her eyes. "One of the men said he would be getting rid of her."

45

Scott rallied his team together in the briefing room as a matter of urgency.

"We've got a situation. Jenna Wade was abducted this morning. From the witness statement, there's a suggestion that some harm will come to her. It's now a priority that we locate her. I've got extra uniformed patrols combing the area for a dark car, possibly an Audi."

Sian interrupted, putting down her phone. "Guv, Murat Ahmeti, whom the Manchester officers have identified as the ringleader, has disappeared off the radar and gone to ground. Local intelligence suggests he's on his way down to Brighton to do a swap. We've got no idea how many girls are with him or whether a swap will actually take place. For all we know, he could be heading into London. Or even meeting halfway somewhere. Perhaps Jenna's earmarked for the swap?"

Mike nodded. "What better way of getting rid of her than switching her with the gang in Manchester? By the time she gets up there, she'll be indoctrinated."

Scott paused as he looked at the whiteboard. Jenna Wade's piercing light blue eyes stared back hauntingly at him. He knew that time was fast running out for her. He was annoyed with himself. They should have placed her in a more secure accommodation. He'd screwed up for not taking the threat to her life seriously enough.

Is she going to pay the price for my misjudgement?

Raj questioned, "Yes, but why Jenna though? She's not far enough down the process. Why take her before she's ready?"

Scott replied, "Because she's a liability. Johnny said as much in the interview. Or maybe Ardit Gashi's associates need to take an extra girl because we've rescued two other girls at the property."

Raj frowned. "But if you know we're on to you, why go ahead with the swap?"

"From his record, the character in Manchester is a serious player. The Brighton connection wouldn't want to let him down or get on the wrong side of him. Maybe it's too late to call it off?" Scott concluded.

"What next, guv?" Mike asked.

"I wish I knew... We play a waiting game now. Johnny gave us a location for where swaps have taken place before. We stake out that location."

The meeting ended, and Abby ahead of him had stopped in the corridor, halfway to her desk. She looked deeply troubled by her thoughts.

Scott caught up with her, grabbing her arm. "Abby, you okay?"

"Can't believe she's still just a kid. It's like she's lived her whole life already," she said harshly. It was clear Abby was fighting to control the anger simmering inside, likely feeling her own frustration that she'd let Jenna down.

"Listen, Abby, you couldn't have done anything more; this isn't your fault. You brought her in; you tried to warn her –"

Abby cut him off. "Yes, but I didn't try hard enough."

"Listen, Johnny did a good job on her. He made her fall in

love. He showed her affection and approval that she'd never had from anyone else. Jenna's fourteen, and she was flattered by this cool eighteen-year-old with cash and charm who could have been with anyone, but he wanted her. You can't compete with hormones."

Abby shrugged. "I know you're right. I just wish I could have shown her where it was all heading. Maybe we should have gone a little heavier on Jenna. Nothing too intense, but we should have shown her how it ends. We should have shown her what happened to Libby Stevens. Maybe that could have got through to her."

"Hindsight is a wonderful thing, Abby, but we don't have time for what-ifs. We can still help her."

Scott left Abby and headed off to DCI Harvey's office to debrief her on the latest.

When he got back to his desk, an email from forensics had arrived and turned the screw on the players even more.

Scott sat back in his chair, a mixture of relief and sadness washing over him as he read one important line.

The laboratory analysis on blood samples found on the cellar floor in the Unicorn pub and the traces of blood on one pair of pliers found in the same location match those of Libby Stevens.

46

Scott was encouraged by recent developments, getting the boost he needed to keep pushing, to keep seeking justice. He finally felt closer to wrapping up the Libby Stevens case. The vile crimes committed against her in the final few hours of her life had become clear. He had hoped that her death had been quick, to ease his own conscience. However, with the evidence staring back at him on the computer screen, his hopes now disappeared into a dark quagmire.

His morning had started on a bad note. Losing a victim was one thing, but Abby looked ready to heap more trouble on his shoulders, as she hastily knocked on his door before entering.

"Guv, Gashi was sprung from the remand van taking him from the magistrates' court to Lewes prison."

Scott sat upright, his eyes wide. He shook his head in disbelief. "What details have we got?"

"Gashi appeared in front of the magistrates this morning. He was denied bail and carted off in a GEO van. They got as far as the junction of Lewes Road and Coldean Lane. A motorcycle and a car pulled up alongside them. Three men jumped out armed with a sawn-off shotgun, baseball bat, and a pickaxe. They smashed the driver's window, threatened to shoot the driver. He was forced out, made to open the van and release Gashi under duress. They got him and sped off towards Lewes."

"That's bloody terrific!" Scott fumed. "What about the others?"

"Renshaw and Wright also had bail denied, but they weren't sprung," Abby said, shaking her head.

"That would explain why Wright kept saying he'd be out soon. He assumed he'd be sprung... Unfortunately for him, it didn't work out that way. How's the driver?"

Abby was leaning against the door frame. "He's shaken up, but both of the guards are okay. We've got armed officers on the scene, and they are making their way towards Lewes, with uniformed officers taking witness statements."

"Someone has obviously been feeding information on Gashi's movements – the most likely suspect is his solicitor, who would have been present at court today. Track him down and give him a hard time, see how much he knows. They must've had bodies close by, ready to go if the opportunity arose."

Abby nodded.

Scott added, "I'm about to interview the driver of the Ducato van with Mike, so keep me updated, and I'll catch up with you afterwards."

47

Scott was making his way down to the interview suite when a familiar voice called to him. He turned to see Matt Allan, the senior SOCO officer, headed for him at speed, waving a thin brown file above his head. He was puffing hard by the time he caught up with Scott.

"I see your exercise regime is paying off," Scott teased. "At this rate you will be able to jog ten yards without getting out of breath."

"If I were you, I wouldn't give up the day job because your jokes suck."

"You're probably right. Anyway, how can I help? I'm about to go and interview a suspect, the one driving the Ducato van that your team has been poring over."

"Good timing, then," he said, holding up the brown file again. "We've been able to identify a match on the blood that we found on the chair leg... It's Libby Stevens's. The blunt instrument used to inflict her injuries was more than likely the chair leg." Matt grimaced.

Even though it was great news, Scott felt a tinge of sadness as more details about her death became known.

Without a response from Scott, Matt continued, "The towels and blankets had traces of human blood on them. They match those of Libby as well, so I suspect she was wrapped in them before being disposed of. But we found more than one blood type."

Scott was all ears now. A seemingly routine stop on a van was revealing the final pieces of this case.

"The chair leg had a second trace of blood on it. When we ran it through the system, it was a match for Christine Newland. I think you've found the murder weapon and possibly the assailant as well. Prints we found on the leg came back as a match for someone on the system: Robert Shaw."

The results confirmed that the two cases of Libby Stevens and Christine Newland were connected. From the forensic evidence, it suggested that both Libby and Christina had been killed with the same weapon.

Armed with new evidence, Scott made his way to the interview room where the owner of the vehicle, Robert Shaw, was sitting on one side of the desk. Mike sat opposite him. A mental health worker was in the seat beside the suspect.

Robert Shaw had waived his right to legal representation and was talking nonsensically to himself when brought in. The unusual behaviour had led to a request for the police doctor. The doctor had concluded that Shaw did indeed have a mild case of borderline personality disorder that became problematic under stress but was controlled through medication.

So much for *That's all in the past now. I've done my time.*

"Mr Shaw, what's your current occupation?" Scott asked.

Shaw didn't reply, looking nervously around the room. He looked at the mental health worker, an Afro-Caribbean woman in her mid-thirties, and nodded enthusiastically at her. Scott couldn't quite figure out why.

"Mr Shaw, for the tape, what is your occupation?" Scott asked again.

This time Shaw faced him, smiling and shrugging. "I'm an odd-job man," he replied flatly.

"Robert, we would like to talk to you about the contents of your van, in particular a chair leg that was found in the rear compartment. Is it yours?"

Shaw paused before speaking. "No. I found it and picked it up. I thought it might be useful."

"In what way would it be useful?" Scott enquired.

Shaw shrugged again. "I don't know, but I do lots of handyman work... Maybe I'll have a job that needs a chair leg."

"Robert, there were bloodstains found on the chair leg and on the towels and blankets in the rear of your van. Could you explain how they came to have blood on them?" Mike asked.

The man shrugged a third time, either unwilling or unable to provide a suitable explanation as to how they came to be in his possession. "It was dark when I found the chair leg. Maybe it already had blood on it and that's how it came to be on everything else."

"And where did you find the chair leg?" Scott asked, knowing what the response would be.

"I don't know. I just found it somewhere around town."

Scott said, "For the time being, we're going to be keeping you here in custody whilst we arrange to search your house. Do you understand?"

Shaw said nothing more, nodding once in agreement, perhaps realising the consequences for him arising from what they'd find there.

After concluding the interview, Scott and Mike made their way back to the CID office. Mike grabbed a coffee from the drinks machine en route. Scott opted for a bottle of still water on this occasion.

"What did you make of him, guv? He didn't seem all there."

"Bit of a waste of time, if I'm being honest. He clearly does have some mental health issues, which may have contributed to his vague answers. But he was clearly giving us the runaround in relation to how the chair leg came into his possession and what it was used for. That's why I terminated the interview early. It makes more sense for us to search his place and see what we find. Then we can reinterview him."

Scott stopped by Abby's desk and pinched her arm lightly.

"Oi, that hurt! That's assault, you know," she said, rubbing her arm.

"Any update on Gashi?"

"Officers traced the car to Kingston just south of Lewes. The car was abandoned there. No further update on where they went from there. We're checking CCTV in the area."

"And his solicitor?"

"Claims he didn't know anything about it. Reckons he's just as horrified as we are that Gashi's absconded."

Scott looked around the office. "Where are the others?"

"Freshfield Way. Raj is over there at the moment on observation. Sian can take over a little later. She's gone home for a change of clothes."

"Okay, I'll be in my office if you need me. I need to arrange a search warrant for Shaw's place ASAP."

48

Scott's arrival at Shaw's property seemed to stir up a lot more interest than on his earlier visit. The arrival of a marked patrol car no doubt contributed to that. In this part of town, the presence of the police suggested one of two things: either a crime had been committed, or someone was about to be arrested, which was a common occurrence.

On this occasion, the door didn't need forcing in. As part of Shaw's arrest, they had confiscated his personal items. His car keys also contained the keys to his front door.

Scott was hit by a damp, musty smell, no doubt from a lack of ventilation. All the officers put on latex gloves. Scott instructed uniformed officers to start looking upstairs. Top of their search list were laptops, computers, mobile phones, photos – anything that would help link Shaw to the murders of Libby Stevens and Christine Newland.

The ground floor of the property consisted of a small lounge-cum-diner, which Scott estimated to be no longer than fifteen feet. To the rear of the property was a small, cramped galley kitchen. Judging by the mess that lay strewn across the kitchen work surface, Shaw lived off convenience food. The man's staple diet appeared to be baked beans, half a loaf of bread, which had the first signs of blue mould creeping in from the edges, and Walkers crisps.

The electric hob looked as if it hadn't been cleaned in years, stained brown, with crusty, dried-on spills. The floor was grey and dirty.

Pushing with the tip of his shoe, Scott rubbed away the dirt on one floor tile to reveal what was once a white square lino tile with a black speckle. Scott rummaged through the kitchen drawers. Kitchen utensils were mixed in with shopping receipts dating back more than six months. Scott flicked through a bunch of expired food saving coupons that were common in the drawers of many kitchen households up and down the country.

As he wandered back into the lounge, he found Abby crouching down, flicking through several porn magazines.

"It's a bit early in the morning for you to be flicking through porn, isn't it?"

Abby turned her nose up. "This is a disgusting job!" Some of the pages in the magazines were stuck together. She heaved. "I think I'm going to be sick."

"Looks like Shaw's been busy," Scott replied.

"It's not so much that he's been busy, it's what he's been using that's more the issue," Abby replied, holding up several copies of *Teens Untamed*. "He seems to enjoy getting off over younger girls, which fits his MO." With a look of disgust on her face, she pinched the edges of the copies and placed them in large, clear plastic evidence bags.

The upstairs of the property didn't fare much better, the threadbare dirty carpets continuing the theme that started downstairs. The small landing had three doors coming off it. To the front, a main bedroom, to the rear, a second bedroom, which in reality was nothing more than a six-foot-square box room, and a small poky bathroom. Scott never understood how estate agents got away with calling a box room a bedroom when you could barely fit in a bed, let alone anything else.

"Anything of interest?" Scott asked one of the officers who was sifting through boxes haphazardly stacked in the box room. There was an assortment of clothing scattered around the floor, and judging by the lack of accessibility, Scott assumed it was a room that was rarely used.

"Nothing of interest, sir. Most of the boxes," he said, pointing in the corner of the room, "have got books in them, clothes that've been stuffed in, and some household knick-knacks. The bathroom's clean too... Well, not clean in that sense, but nothing worth bagging up."

"Okay, keep looking. There's more here, I'm sure of it." Scott ventured into the front bedroom. He was amazed at how some people lived. Judging by the stained and ingrained dirt, the bedding hadn't been washed in months. It was loosely falling off the end of the bed, with more clothes scattered around the floor. He could see small particles of floating dust caught in the sunlight that was now starting to irritate his nostrils. There was a sense of untidiness and filth in all directions.

He found the other officer leant over a small bedside cabinet, picking through the contents of the top drawer. "Sir, there's a laptop just under the bed here, and I found a piece of paper resting on it," she said, handing the evidence bag over to Scott.

On it was scribbled:

Newhaven 3pm.

Scott's mind was whirring – was this the time and location of a potential swap? Or a drop? It was also the ferry terminal. Was this the time of a sailing?

"There's some other stuff pushed under the bed, sir," the officer continued, pulling out three more porn magazines. Each of the covers had young models dressed up to look like teenagers in saucy school uniforms, posing in erotic positions.

"Don't tell me, some of the pages are stuck together?"

"I'm afraid so, sir. There's also what appears to be female underwear, namely several pairs of knickers with little cherries and daisies on them. They appear to be crunched up and a little crusty, if you know what I mean."

Scott was beginning to get a deeper understanding of Robert Shaw from the evidence.

Filthy place, filthy mind, a loner; he likes to be in the company of children, which is why he's been found lurking outside school gates and youth clubs. He gains sexual gratification from looking at images of teens. No coincidence that he lives a short distance from a children's playground and is going to some lengths to conceal his depravity.

The more Scott thought about this, the stronger he felt about Shaw's involvement in the trafficking ring. He had done his best to put them off his tracks by pleading his innocence when they'd first visited him. However, as Scott stood in Shaw's lair, the evidence was too great, and the tide was turning against him. A holler from the officer in the small box room dragged Scott away from his thoughts.

He noticed the ashen look on the officer's face as he stepped back from a box he'd been examining on the floor. Pushing back the flaps on the box for Scott, it revealed a small white coffee jar. It wasn't the jar itself that alarmed him, but what appeared to be bloodstained prints on the outside. Carefully holding the jar from the base to avoid disturbing the prints, he slowly prised off the cork lid. What he found inside took him a moment to process.

Cotton wool had been stuffed into the bottom half of the

jar. Resting on top were what appeared to be dark brown rubbery objects. With the help of the officer, who shone his torch into the jar, the full horror of the discovery soon hit home. Scott was looking at what appeared to be a tongue and some small round circular pieces of flesh, which Scott thought resembled the look and shape of nipples.

"Found these, too," the officer said, reaching into the box once again and pulling out a Dior watch and phone that were stuffed in amongst the clothes.

Scott examined the back of the watch. "Love Alan". They were vital pieces of evidence that sealed Shaw's fate and sent lightning bolts of revulsion and horror through Scott.

BACK IN THE OFFICE, word soon spread about the crucial evidence discovered at Shaw's property. Scott was certain that Shaw was complicit in two murders; he had little room to wriggle out.

Having reviewed, videoed, bagged and documented the evidence at Shaw's house, both Scott and Abby were still affected by what they'd discovered there. At one point Abby had had to leave to get some fresh air outdoors or risk throwing up.

As police officers, they were used to seeing the aftermath of horrendous crimes, dead bodies and body parts, but the evidence surfacing in this investigation was affecting their emotional and moral core. It was all too easy to be told to put their emotions to one side, as they had a job to do. But they were human beings nevertheless, affected by circumstances that hit everyone: grief, tragedy and the desperate plight of the vulnerable.

Several large bags of evidence were dispatched to Matt's team in forensics, with an urgent request to process them whilst they had Shaw in custody for twenty-four hours. His laptop had been sent to the high-tech unit for analysis. Scott was hoping there would be incriminating evidence linking him to other key members in the ring, in particular Johnny Wright and Ardit Gashi.

49

Shaw was back in the interview room, this time looking decidedly more uncomfortable as he shot nervous glances between Scott and Abby, who sat silently with their arms crossed.

Scott was determined to put Shaw under significant strain. He desperately needed him to crack; the man needed to be sweating from every pore. As far as Scott was concerned, this would be the last day Shaw walked a free man. The evidence he'd found at the property left no doubt in Scott's mind that Shaw was sick and depraved and involved in the two deaths.

The criminal justice system was there for a reason – to bring to justice those who had committed the most heinous of crimes. In Scott's opinion, crimes against underage children ranked at the top. A lengthy custodial sentence would be too lenient for Shaw.

"Robert, could you explain how you came to have in your possession a small coffee jar with what appears to be human remains in it?" Scott asked, holding up a picture of the jar in question.

"Dunno."

"For the purposes of the tape, I'm showing Mr Shaw a picture of a Dior watch with the inscription *Love Alan* on the back. How did this come to be in your possession?"

Shaw shrugged and smirked. "Won it in a Christmas cracker."

"Do you enjoy looking at magazines of naked teenage girls? Does it turn you on?"

Abby stayed silent during this exchange, choosing wisely to make notes. Scott worked on Shaw from the edges, bringing him closer and closer to the centre.

"You see, here's my theory," Scott said. "I believe that you are involved in the murders of Libby Stevens and Christine Newland. Am I correct?"

"What if I was?" he said with a grunt. "There's plenty more like them."

"Like who?"

"Girls... women... slags... whores... They want it." He smiled a sickening smile that exposed his yellow-stained teeth.

"What do they want, Robert?" Scott asked.

"They want sex. They want to be fucked. They want me to abuse them." Shaw closed his eyes and inhaled deeply. The words alone appeared to be arousing him.

Scott flicked on his phone and opened a video that he'd taken of specific video clips on Shaw's phone. He turned the screen to the accused and pressed play.

The room filled with the piercing cries and screams of a girl shouting, "Please stop... please..."

Shaw sat up straight.

What followed were further guttural screams as the video played out the systematic torture of Libby Stevens.

Abby closed her eyes for a few moments.

The video of Libby Stevens played on, her spreadeagled,

naked, draped over a beer keg. Her wrists had been secured with chains attached to the wall. Gashi was forcibly inserting the chair leg between her legs. The sight of blood trailing down the insides of her thighs sent a cold shiver through Scott and also Abby. He saw her grip her own thighs under the table.

Scott desperately wanted to switch off the phone; he had no desire to put himself through this again. Bile hit the back of his throat once more. He swallowed it. Scott needed to stay steadfast; he needed to break this man, for Libby's sake as much as his own.

As the video continued to play, laughter rang out from those present in the cellar. The perpetrators taunted Libby and egged on Gashi to inflict more pain on the defenceless girl. Her screams mixed with bouts of pained crying. The extra encouragement fuelled Gashi's rage as he viciously pulled out Libby's fingernails one by one, unleashing a torrent of chilling screams that turned Scott's stomach.

She was just fifteen.

Her constant pleas fell on deaf ears.

"I promise I won't say anything" was all she could muster before she slipped into unconsciousness. Gashi hit her with the chair leg, a dull crack on her skull, the final act that silenced her, ending her misery – ending her life.

"How did you come to have that chair leg in your possession?" Scott said, his voice controlled but tinged with anger.

Whilst the video had been playing, Shaw had kept his eyes firmly closed. A slight smile on his face suggested he'd been playing back the whole scene, a scene that was enjoyable in his twisted mind.

Shaw opened his eyes. "Gashi asked me to get rid of the evidence. I took her to the marina and slung her over the wall."

"If he asked you to get rid of the evidence, why did you

still have in your possession the chair leg and her tongue? I assume it's her tongue?"

Shaw nodded. "I kept them as souvenirs, presents for me, something that reminds me of a very enjoyable experience." He paused for a moment, pulling on some more memories. "She had lovely soft skin, small firm tits... They were lovely to touch." Shaw was breathing hard now. His eyes closed once again, and he licked his lips, fantasies taking him into a different world that stirred his perverse senses.

Scott had come across many people in his job, but this vile predator ranked amongst the worst. He was getting off on recalling the memories.

"Who else was present?" Scott asked.

Shaw paused for a moment, resting his chin on his hand. "Me, the landlord, Gashi and two other blokes I didn't know. They were associates of Gashi."

"And Christine Newland? How did her blood end up on the chair leg?" Scott asked.

Shaw shook his head slowly and smiled. "She was a very silly woman. She came to warn me off."

His statement piqued Scott's curiosity. "To warn you off?"

Shaw laughed; the smell of his stale breath assaulted Scott's nostrils. "I was supposed to be meeting her girl, Lucy. Then she turned up, telling me to stay away from her daughter, and that she would report me to the police. She called me a filthy pervert... She couldn't get away with saying that, could she? That's not a nice thing to say when I was going to show Lucy a good time."

It was starting to make sense. "So you're Johnny from the chat room?"

"Yeah, it was easy to hide behind Johnny. I knew if anyone found out about the conversation, they would think it's Johnny Wright. I would get away with it," he proudly said.

"What happened next?"

"She tried to punch me, she was swearing, telling me to stay away, so I hit her... I hit her hard, and she went down. I went back to the van, got my Stanley knife and the chair leg. I hit her over the head... hard... then kept hitting her." He smiled, shook his head. "Boy, her head was smashed in big time. She stopped breathing. But she looked fine, just like her daughter, a real good looker. Proper MILF. She turned me on, gave me a right hard-on when I touched her. Her hair smelt fresh, her perfume... hmm. She had big breasts, big nipples... so I took them."

Scott sat back, revulsed by this lowlife.

50

The Shaw interview had gone on late. After, Scott stayed even later at his desk. His mind was spinning. He was wired, angry and frustrated.

With the door closed, the sanctuary of his office gave him the space to process what he'd heard. He sat there staring at one spot on the wall, his fists clenched, his lips nothing but a thin line. He couldn't recall the last time an interviewee had got to him so much. The man was pure evil.

He'd cancelled his meetup with Cara at the last minute. Tired and hungry, Scott headed home, where he managed a few slices of toast spread with copious amounts of marmalade before sleep took hold of him and he crashed on the sofa.

Scott slowly stirred. Light was streaming in around the edges of the curtains in the lounge. His neck ached – a price he paid for not making it to his bed.

Tiredness faded when he soaked in the shower. The water washed away the sleep and grime. The house was quiet without Cara. Scott had been looking forward to seeing her;

he enjoyed her company – she brought a smile to his face. But he'd been no company last night.

Cara was having an effect on him, more than he realised. He loved her laughter. There was something else he loved about her personality that he couldn't quite put his finger on.

She was vibrant, infectious and fun. That was it.

She was fun to be around, and in the short space of time that he'd got to know her, it felt right.

SCOTT PULLED into Freshfield Way and parked up behind Sian's blue Astra. Raj had taken the first watch yesterday, with Sian doing the graveyard shift with Mike. Neither got out of their cars, for fear of being seen. Scott chose instead to talk to them over the police radio.

"Anything to report, guys?"

Sian replied in a groggy, tired voice, "Nope, not a sausage. That was until about an hour ago when a white van drove up and down the road three times. It hasn't come back."

"Okay, I'll take over. Abby will be here in a few minutes with some coffees. You and Mike clock off."

"Think Mike's already beaten you to it; he's practically asleep. The lazy git."

The waiting, the not knowing was something that Scott rarely enjoyed. TV programmes and films often glamorised stake-outs with shoot-outs, fights, and high-speed car chases that left a trail of destruction across a city, but they were anything but glamorous. It usually meant hours of waiting around, often with nothing to show for it – unless it was an intelligence-led operation. But that wasn't always the case. They'd spent more than their fair share of mind-numbing hours waiting around in cars in the middle of winter, hands and feet chilled to the bone.

The coffees Abby brought were a welcome distraction. Together, they watched various goods vehicles trundle in and out of the industrial estate.

Over the course of the next hour the pair sat in silence, just watching, playing the occasional round of I Spy. Abby invariably won due to picking the most abstract objects like a hubcap, a yellow parking sign and a McDonald's food wrapper that whipped around outside, caught in the back-draught of passing vehicles.

A few times, Abby furiously tapped away on her phone keypad for a few seconds before looking up and staring off into the distance.

"What on earth are you doing?" he asked.

She laughed. "It's a crossword app, can't think of anything better to do, so I might as well do this."

Scott raised an eyebrow. "Small things please small minds."

"Stop talking about yourself like that. Besides, you couldn't do this even if you tried!"

"Try me," he challenged.

"Okay, clever clogs, here's a couple I'm stuck on. Twenty-one across, six letters, bungle, starting with *F* and the fourth letter is *L*."

Scott thought for a moment, tapping the steering wheel with his finger. "Foul-up."

Abby growled. "Fluke." Determined to catch him out, she said, "Nine down, five letters, a reproductive cell in the sporagium. Last letter is *E*."

A few seconds later, "Spore," he offered.

Abby sighed loudly. "I hate you!"

Resolute on finding one he couldn't figure out, she scanned her unanswered clues. "One across, user's treatment, five letters, ending with *B*."

"Rehab," he fired back, smiling smugly.

Abby threw the phone onto the dashboard in defeat. "Do you know, you're far too clever for your own good!"

Scott cemented the victory by licking the tip of his finger and chalking it in the air. "Some have it, some don't," he replied, brushing each of his shoulders.

Abby sulked, her arms crossed in defiance. "How's it going with scalpel woman... I mean, Cara?"

"It's going good. Thanks for the lack of genuine interest. We seem to get on really well."

"Going good... or going *really good*?" Abby teased, giving Scott a wink.

"Yeah, wouldn't you like to know?"

"Yes, I would, as I'm not getting any at the moment."

"Listen, the sooner you get yourself a man, the quicker you'll stop asking me questions about my love life. So flipping well get out there and find someone."

"You make it sound as if I can just click my fingers and the man of my dreams will suddenly appear in a puff of smoke in front of me."

Scott knew that Abby would much rather make a joke of a situation than admit how she really felt. "Come on; tell the Love Doctor what's holding you back."

That drew a smile and chuckle from Abby. "Love Doctor... hmm, not sure about that."

"I'm waiting."

She sighed. "I guess I'm scared. Meeting someone would mean so much of my life would change. I've spent the last couple of years on my own, and I'm used to it. I have no one else to worry about except the kids. And let's be honest, how many people outside of the job really understand the nature of our job? I'm a copper; we *are* the job. Me and him would be passing ships in the night. The early shifts, the late shifts, the countless hours we stay long after our shifts have finished. Then you go home, and you still have work stuff going on inside your head. In the little spare time I do have, I've got the chores, the kids, and I've *got* to get to the gym. I'd be a bloody nightmare to live with. And I'm not sure if I want all the aggro again."

"Well, to quote a Chinese fortune cookie, 'If you don't try, you'll never know,' which makes sense to me."

"Chinese fortune cookie, my ass."

"Listen, Abby, I'm not giving you a hard time, but I'm talking to you as a friend not your boss. Take some action, get your profile up on Match.com and see what happens. Stop making bloody excuses."

She rolled her eyes. "Yes, you can just imagine the weirdos who would seek me out when they find out I'm a copper." She mocked in a deep male voice, "'You going to wear your uniform for me, luv?' 'You can cuff me any time.' 'You show me your truncheon and I'll show you mine.' Ugh! And that's just for starters."

The conversation stalled as Abby turned to look out the window, deep in thought.

Scott broke the silence and nudged Abby in the ribs. "Looks like we got company." He nodded ahead.

About two hundred yards down the street, two transit vans had come to a stop. They had parked tail to tail but with enough space for their rear doors to open. Both occupants got out, greeting each other with a handshake before looking around nervously at the occupants of any cars or vehicles that passed them.

They both opened their rear cargo doors, creating a corridor between the two vans to block any exchange from prying eyes.

Scott and Abby sat up, alert. Scott switched on his engine. The waiting had paid off.

"You ready?" he said to her.

A nod from Abby was the only confirmation he needed.

Scott put the car in gear and accelerated towards the vans, stopping nose to nose with one of them to ensure it couldn't move. Abby was already out the door and running, with Scott a few paces behind.

"Police! Stay where you are!" Abby shouted as she came round one side of the vans, with Scott taking the other side. He thought they'd try to run or put up a fight, but they didn't.

It was too easy. Something wasn't right.

The two drivers froze, each raising their arms in surrender a little too quickly. Scott grabbed one man whilst Abby grabbed the other. They gave each man a swift kick behind the knees, to bring them to their knees. It gave the officers a small advantage, allowing them space and time to cuff the suspects.

It was only when Scott glanced in each van that the simplicity of the arrest made sense.

The vans were empty.

They'd been stitched up.

51

Scott stormed into his office, throwing his police radio on the desk and thumping the top of his chair.

"They had us. They knew we were on to them. They set the whole thing up and made us look like right muppets!"

Abby was leaning in his doorway, her arms folded. "It happens, guv; it's not the first time we've been given the runaround. If you think about it, we have most of the key players in this trafficking and prostitution ring, so it's not surprising they knew we were on their trail."

Scott knew that Abby was making perfect sense, but it didn't stop him feeling frustrated at the wasted man-hours over the last twenty-four hours. This wasn't the only case that his team had to deal with, but he'd prioritised his resources, expecting a successful outcome. He would now have to go and justify this to DCI Harvey, something he wasn't looking forward to.

THE DCI HAD JUST COME out of a meeting with the superintendent when she saw Scott loitering by her door. She walked past him and, with a nod, invited him in.

"What went wrong?" she said, leaning back in her chair and resting her arms on the armrests. She was staring at Scott.

He stood in the DCI's office. On most occasions she would offer him a seat. But he was always left standing when she was angry. The other hint to her annoyance was her furrowed brows.

"We got stitched up. Plain and simple. Gashi knows we're on to him, and this was him sticking two fingers up at us. We're on a wild goose chase, ma'am." Scott sighed.

The DCI pursed her lips as she weighed up their options. "Listen, Scott, yes, I agree it was a waste of time. However, I get the impression that Gashi is a very shrewd operator. Have you considered the fact that this morning was a deliberate diversion?"

"Diversion?"

The DCI nodded. "Yes, a diversion to take our resources away from what he was really doing. If he was desperate enough to put on a diversion this morning, it means he's running scared and knows we're on his tail *and* closing in. From what I can gather, the Manchester contact has just gone to ground. We have no intelligence to suggest he's here in Brighton or making his way to Brighton... Agreed?" She held her hands in front of her whilst keeping her elbows on the armrests.

Scott had to agree with her hypothesis. "It's plausible to think that Gashi still has Jenna Wade and Rishi Mehta in his possession."

"Exactly. They're his prized assets at the moment. They could also be his bargaining tool... his get-out-of-jail card, so to speak, to use if he ever gets hemmed into a corner. We need to find him," she said, raising an eyebrow, "and you know exactly where you can get the information from."

SCOTT BRIEFLY POPPED BACK to his desk to gather his case files ahead of another interview with Robert Shaw. Whilst he'd been in with the DCI, several emails had arrived in his inbox. The first was from Tim Coburn, the forensic computer examiner. He was informing Scott that useful information had been recovered from all the laptops, including the most recent one from Robert Shaw. Scott decided he would take a detour on the way down to the interview suite and stop by Tim's desk.

The other email that piqued his interest was from the forensic unit. They had rushed through analysis on the evidence from Robert Shaw's property. As Scott scrolled further down the email, the evidence clearly highlighted the depravity of the man.

The first bit of analysis confirmed that, following DNA swabs taken from Robert Shaw, DNA profiling confirmed a match between Shaw's DNA and the semen traces found in the crunched-up knickers. Scott shrugged at this news; it was always likely that would have been the case.

The rest of the email was far more pertinent to his investigation.

DNA profiling had confirmed that the tongue found in the coffee jar belonged to Libby Stevens. Forensics also confirmed that the other human body parts found in the coffee jar were indeed nipples. DNA profiling confirmed a match with Christine Newland.

Scott slumped in his chair. The vital elements of his case were now complete. He knew the murderers for both cases, two of whom were detained; he had the accomplices and the motives. He should have felt relieved. But he felt deflated.

Even though the perpetrators who committed these crimes were going to be prosecuted, it wasn't going to bring back Libby Stevens or Christine Newland. Nor was justice going to replace the brutal final moments in both of their lives.

Social services might never be able to identify the relatives of Libby Stevens. But in Christine Newland's case, her family was going to experience further grief as the final moments in her life were played out in court.

52

As Scott expected, Tim Coburn was elbow-deep in computer paper and various electronic gadgets. Seeing Scott arrive, he frantically scrabbled about his desk, trying to find the relevant paperwork that Scott would be demanding.

"I've got the information you requested. I found lots of distinctive messages between the laptop belonging to Robert Shaw and Johnny Wright on the darknet via a private network. However, there were no messages or evidence of any chat history between Johnny Wright's laptop and Lucy Newland's laptop. There was, however, chat history, as we know already, between Robert Shaw's laptop and Lucy Newland's laptop. So it's fairly likely that Robert Shaw was using a fake profile in the name of Johnny to communicate with Lucy."

"Okay, that's really helpful to know. Thanks for speeding that job through, Tim."

Scott's opinion of the analyst was changing. When he needed the goods, Tim produced them.

Maybe he isn't such a nerdy plank after all.

Scott and Abby found themselves once again facing Robert Shaw. The lack of ventilation coupled with a particularly hot day left the room feeling stuffy and claustrophobic. Scott released a shirt button and pulled down his tie before proceeding to roll up his sleeves. His sweaty arms stuck to the desk as he leant forward to look Shaw in the eyes.

Shaw was still sneering at the officers. Scott's opinion of him had changed again. He wasn't a lowlife: he was the filth found at the bottom of the pond.

After taking a short swig of water, Scott cleared his throat. "Mr Shaw, we will be charging you with the online grooming of a child and the murder of Christine Newland. Not that it matters to you, but we have two vulnerable girls out there that we need to find. They have families and loved ones who want them back. If you're willing to cooperate with us, we will make sure that the CPS know that you assisted us in this matter."

"Why would I help you now?" he replied, folding his arms, his shoulders twitching.

"Conscience?" Scott offered.

That suggestion was met with a roar of laughter. Shaw tipped his head back. "Bit late for that, ain't it?" he said, rolling his eyes.

Scott decided to change course. He folded his arms to mimic Shaw's defensive posture, a look of curiosity on his face. "You know it surprises me that the people who should be sitting in that chair," Scott said, pointing to where Shaw was sitting, "are the very same people you're protecting. They will get away scot-free, and you'll end up doing time for them. It hardly seems fair, does it? And you know what they do to nonces inside, don't you?"

Shaw remained apathetic. His eyes were firmly fixed on

Abby, his mouth becoming moist as his sick perverted mind fantasised over her. His eyes focused on her breasts. Shaw placed one hand on his groin and proceeded to rub his genitals.

Despite every muscle in Abby's body straining, pushing her to launch across the desk and gouge his eyes out in the defence of all women, she remained still.

Scott said, "Mr Shaw, you'll have plenty of time to do that for twenty-three hours a day, seven days a week. Where's Gashi?"

His question seemed to break Shaw's erotic fantasy and bring him back to the present.

Shaw scowled at him, his teeth gritted. "You're too late! In an hour he'll be gone." He laughed, waving his arm gently in front of him. "Sailing away."

Scott and Abby exchanged a glance. They concluded the interview and raced through the corridors of the station.

Scott shouted at Abby to arrange for two fast patrol cars with pursuit drivers to meet them downstairs. Scott notified Mike and Sian of the plan, both of whom had just come on shift.

The race was on to get to Newhaven Ferry Port by three p.m.

53

As they raced out of the station, Abby was fuming at Shaw's attitude. "Shaw's a sick bastard."

"We've seen worse."

"Yes, but the way he was looking at me made my skin crawl."

Scott and Abby jumped in the second of two marked cars. Both screeched out of the station, their sirens blaring, the noise bouncing off the tall nearby buildings. They both hung on to the grab handles in the rear of the vehicle as it tore down William Street before turning right on to Edward Street towards the Old Steine, weaving around cars, throwing Scott and Abby from one side to the other.

Normally it would take about thirty minutes to get to Newhaven. In a marked police car, with a pursuit driver at the wheel, they'd make it in fifteen minutes. The DI had already radioed ahead to inform the Newhaven port authorities to be on the lookout for two young girls and two men of Eastern European extraction. He also had local police units racing to the scene. One way or another, they were both determined to get the girls back.

The car took the first left off the roundabout in front of Palace Pier at such speed that Abby wondered how they managed to stay in one piece. She exchanged nervous glances with him. It had been a while since she'd been in a pursuit car that was being pushed to its limits by an advanced police driver.

The traffic along Marina Parade was flowing but heavy. As the sirens from both cars wailed, unprepared drivers swerved in all directions, some unsure of Highway Code protocols when they saw the blue lights looming up fast in their rear-view mirrors.

This often amused Abby when she saw the sheer look of terror and confusion on drivers' faces when emergency vehicles appeared. He'd seen drivers mount pavements or press their horns nervously, infuriated that the driver in front hadn't moved. He'd even witnessed drivers just freeze and not do anything, hoping that they'd suddenly become invisible.

Abby's phone rang. Reaching into her handbag with one hand wasn't an easy task at the best of times. Doing it in the back of a police car at high speed was nigh impossible.

She didn't recognise the number but answered nevertheless. "Hello?" she shouted over the din of the sirens and police radio chatter. "Hello? I can't hear you. Who is it?"

Abby's eyes widened as the caller whispered her name again. "It's Jenna Wade. Help!"

She thumped Scott's arm a few times to get his attention.

"Jenna, where are you?" she said.

Jenna was whispering, making it hard to decipher her responses. "I'm trapped in the back of a van. Please help; I feel drowsy."

"Jenna, who else is there?"

"It's just me and another girl."

"What's her name?" Abby could hear a muffled few words on the other end of the line.

"Her name's Rishi."

A bolt of adrenaline surged through her like an electric shock. She mouthed the name *Rishi* to Scott, who was sitting tensely.

"Can you tell me what you can see?" she asked Jenna.

The reply was faint. Abby tapped the front seat to motion for the officer to stop. The lead car with Mike and Sian raced on. Scott got on the radio and gave them an update as to why they'd stopped, and told them to hold their position.

"Jenna, I need you to tell me what you can see," Abby pushed.

"There's no windows," she replied in a hushed tone.

"What can you hear?"

There was a lengthy pause before Jenna replied, "I can hear seagulls... wait! I can hear sirens... yes, sirens, and they're getting louder. No... no," she yelled. "They're going; it's fading away. It's gone. No, stop!" She began to cry.

Scott leant forward and spoke to the driver. "Drive farther up and keep your sirens on," he instructed before giving Abby a nod.

Abby asked, "Jenna, what can you hear now?"

"Erm... I can hear more sirens... there's more sirens," she replied frantically. "Please help."

"It's the marina!" Scott yelled.

54

The patrol car roared off again; the marina was just below them to the right. The road rose, leaving the outskirts of Brighton and the tall apartment blocks in their elevated position far behind them.

It wasn't going to be the easiest place to search for the girls. The area covered a large plot with an overwhelming mix of social attractions, from bars and restaurants to cinemas, a casino and a health club. It also had a thriving marina with an assortment of marine vessels coming and going. Searching for a needle in a haystack came to Scott's mind.

The dilemma for him and his team was how to locate the girls without drawing attention to them and scaring off those who had brought them here. This in itself was going to be hard with four plain-clothes officers and four uniformed officers. The likelihood was that Gashi or others unknown would see them first and evade capture, leaving the girls in a perilous position if they were not found quickly.

"What're we going to do, guv?" Abby asked.

Scott didn't reply; he knew the only way to locate the girls was to use the police siren as a locating beacon that Jenna could use to guide them in. It was a risky gamble. Not only would it draw significant attention to them but would for sure alert the girls' captors. He needed to act fast and make an executive decision – a decision that would have far-reaching consequences for the girls, Gashi and Scott's career if it went wrong.

Scott assigned one patrol car to cover the exit route and deployed officers to stop and search all vehicles leaving the area. He dispatched another officer to find the marina management team, who could scan the mooring points for any signs of suspicious activity.

Mike and Sian followed on foot behind the patrol car with Scott and Abby in it. Scott felt the best option was to stop at certain intervals, sound off the siren and ask Jenna for feedback.

The first occasion occurred outside the Subway takeaway food bar, when Jenna replied that she could vaguely hear it. The next stop was by the McDonald's fast-food outlet, to which Jenna replied that the sound was louder and therefore nearer.

Scott felt hopeful, but each time the siren sounded, it attracted more public interest, something that made Scott uneasy. Gashi could be amongst the throngs of people and already be making good his escape. They couldn't scan every person; there were just too many of them.

He was starting to regret his plan of action but had little other choice. Flooding the area with officers would have made the situation worse and attracted far too much interest and perhaps even started a panic. Speed was of the essence.

Scott alerted the officer to sound the siren again when they'd reached the end of the road between the David Lloyd leisure club and the car park.

Again Jenna confirmed that they were close now, a mix of panic and excitement in her voice.

As they rounded the back of the club, the siren sounded once again, to which Jenna screamed down the phone, "I'm here... you're right here!"

To the right of them were a few parking spaces. Most were empty, but a small white Citroën Berlingo van was parked beside a red Vauxhall Astra car that had seen better days.

"That's it," Scott bellowed as he and Abby exited the patrol car at the same time.

Abby was banging on the rear door of the van. "Jenna, are you in there?"

"Yes," a faint voice came back.

Scott searched around, looking for something to prise open the door. An industrial bin close by had the remnants of a shop refit loosely piled up in it. Scott raced over and rummaged around before returning with a long, flat piece of steel that he wedged between the two rear doors.

The doors wouldn't budge. Both Scott and the uniformed PC leant into the bar, hoping to prise the door open; it moved but not enough to free the locking mechanism.

An out-of-breath Mike and Sian soon joined them.

"Mike, give us a hand."

The three of them were now leaning hard on the steel bar, causing the van to lean hard to one side.

Without warning, the locking mechanism gave way with a loud clank, components shearing off in all directions. It sent the three officers tumbling to the ground in a heap. The doors flew open and revealed two girls shielding their eyes from the bright sunlight.

They lay on the floor of the van, looking defenceless, curled up in fetal positions. Tears streaked their dirty cheeks. Fear was etched on their faces as they blinked.

Abby knelt inside and smiled. "You're safe, girls, you're safe."

55

Relief engulfed Scott, the knot in his stomach easing. He hadn't been sure if he'd find Rishi Mehta. For all he knew, she could have been taken out of the country earlier. Finding Jenna went some way to vindicating his guilt over letting her down the first time.

Scott and the fellow officers dusted themselves off. They'd only suffered minor abrasions on their hands, elbows and knees that kissed the concrete.

"Abby, call for an ambulance," Scott said. "Jenna looks okay, but is probably suffering from shock. Rishi needs medical attention." He looked at the girl, who appeared to be undernourished, dazed and dehydrated. Her face looked gaunt, her eyes were sunken, and her bare legs displayed evidence of extensive bruising.

Scott knelt next to where Jenna was now sitting at the rear of the van. Her legs were dangling over the edge. "Jenna, this is really important; who brought you here?"

Jenna still seemed to be dazed from her ordeal, her face a mixture of emotions. Everything that she had been led to believe over the past few weeks had been nothing more than an elaborate set of lies. The hope of love, the hope someone would take care of her for the first time in her life, dashed by deceit.

She looked around, trying to get her bearings. She ran a hand through her knotted hair. It was evident to Scott that the abduction had not only been traumatic but had left her wildly confused.

"It... it... was Ardit. He was talking to someone on the phone when we got here. I just heard him say he was preparing the boat to go."

The officers exchanged a series of glances. If they were to reach a satisfactory conclusion, they needed to apprehend Ardit, and they needed to do it fast. For all Scott knew, the sound of the sirens might have already alerted Ardit to their presence, and he'd slipped away.

Scott and Mike raced towards the mooring points, passing all the shops and restaurants that they'd seen earlier on their arrival. Scott was concerned, his mind processing a multitude of likely outcomes. The warm early summer sunshine had brought out the visitors. With so many people around, it was going to be harder to spot Gashi. There was also an overriding concern for the safety of the public in case Gashi did anything rash to protect himself.

The road took them only as far as the first jetty. Scott, Mike and one uniformed officer ran on to the walkway. They were met by the second officer whom Scott had dispatched earlier. He was standing with a thin bespectacled man who introduced himself as Harry Silverman, head of security for Brighton Marina.

Scott introduced himself. "I'm Detective Inspector Baker from Brighton CID. We believe that a suspect is about to leave from a vessel moored here. It's possible that he's looking to reach Dieppe. Do you have details of anyone recorded in your log as leaving today?"

Harry Silverman lifted his glasses and rested them above his eyes so that he could look at his schedule in greater detail. He ran his finger down the page, mumbling to himself.

"I've got one vessel leaving before four p.m. today. Unusual case."

"How's that?"

"Well, the boat was bought a few days ago for cash. Eighteen thousand pounds, to be precise. As you can imagine, we don't often get people coming in here with large sums of cash wishing to buy boats." He shrugged. "They bought a Westerly Pentland 32. Then another chap arrived today just an hour or so ago. He signed some paperwork and then headed off to Asda to get some provisions. I saw him come back about twenty minutes ago and head down there." Silverman pointed in the direction of the long walkway to their left.

"You're saying he's down there now?"

"Well, yes, I'd imagine so. His boat is called *Lela Rose*. He's berthed off the second jetty. Number sixty-four, according to the schedule."

Armed with this information, Scott and the other officers raced down the walkway. The sight of four burly officers running past diners enjoying al fresco dining in the sunshine drew looks of curiosity and concern.

Arriving at the second jetty, Scott saw various boat owners milling around. Some were sharing a joke in small groups. Others were comparing their boats proudly with one another. And the odd one or two were avidly undertaking maintenance tasks on deck.

Scott glanced around to identify the berth numbers.

"Fifty-two... fifty-three..."

Scott didn't need to look much further. The *Lela Rose* was berthed at sixty-four.

Scott and his team didn't have an opportunity to reach the boat. His attention was drawn to a melee happening behind them. At the start of the second jetty, owners were being pushed out of the way as a man sprinted off at speed.

"It's him," Scott shouted.

The officers doubled back and raced back down the jetty. There was more confusion than Scott would have liked. He was really hoping to have taken Gashi by surprise. Instead, Gashi had taken them by surprise and now had the head start.

As they raced back down the walkway, Gashi was trying to slow them down, grabbing chairs from the nearby restaurants and throwing them into the walkway. He was looking for any opportunity to slow down his pursuers as he glanced around, looking for a way out.

Scott was fast gaining ground on Gashi. He could hear the man breathing heavily just a few feet in front of him. The sound of gasps and the occasional scream from passers-by faded into the background as he ran on.

The man was now in touching distance. Scott reached out and made a grab for Gashi by the shoulder. Gashi, clearly in no mood to surrender, rammed his elbow into Scott's face, sending them both crashing to the ground. Scott quickly attempted to get his feet, but Gashi launched him over his shoulder, and he was thrown back down in a judo-style move.

Scott came crashing down, then winced when the full force of Gashi's right fist connected with his jaw. Gashi was offering more resistance than Scott had bargained for as the two thrashed about on the concrete. Gashi repeatedly punched Scott, who was now pinned to the ground, with Scott desperately trying to push him off.

Gashi got to his feet, threatening to stamp on Scott's face. Gashi didn't get the opportunity – he was sent flying as Mike shoulder-charged him. The kinetic energy of a five-foot, eleven-inch ex-soldier shoulder-charging him at full pelt gave

Gashi no hope of retaliating. He lay spreadeagled on the ground, dazed from being hit by a bulldozer.

Scott slowly got to his feet, his head spinning, his nose bleeding, and his pride slightly dented.

"Nick him, Mike. Nick the bastard."

56

The outcome had been a good one for Scott and his team. They had broken a trafficking and teen prostitution ring. They'd apprehended the key players in the ring and rescued girls who were destined for a life of pain, misery and potential death.

"You did well, Scott," DCI Harvey said.

"Thanks, ma'am, but it doesn't feel that way," he replied, nursing a bruised and broken nose and a black eye. "We didn't get everyone... We had a chance to get Korab Gashi, he was in the country, but he gave us the slip. He'd departed earlier than we were led to believe. I screwed up. That note we found at Shaw's property said Newhaven 3 p.m., suggesting that the Gashi brothers and the girls were leaving from Newhaven at that time."

DCI Harvey nodded.

"And as we know, ma'am, the older Gashi brother gave everyone the slip. By the time I alerted Newhaven, he'd already left. When local officers trawled video footage, Korab Gashi was seen boarding the eleven o'clock from Newhaven to Dieppe. Guess he's the one who got away."

"Until next time, Scott. Until next time. He cut it a bit fine this time, but he'll be back, and next time you'll be waiting for him."

SCOTT AND ABBY pulled up a couple of worn plastic visitor chairs, placing them between the beds of Jenna Wade and Rishi Mehta in the children's ward.

Jenna was suffering from dehydration and shock. Rishi was a different case altogether. Her physical scars and bruising would heal. The psychological scars would take longer. She had many weeks, perhaps even months of counselling ahead of her. It was debatable whether her life would ever be anything close to normal. She'd already lost part of her childhood, her innocence stolen, her body abused. A distorted perspective on reality now tinted her view of life. Her trust in adults and men in particular had been broken, which Scott imagined would affect her future relationships. Sympathy for her plight seemed too inadequate.

"I want you both to know that you're safe now," Scott said, addressing both girls. "The men who did this can't hurt you or any other girl ever again."

Jenna was sitting up in bed, fiddling with a tissue that she was wrapping and unwrapping around one of her fingers. Rishi lay silent, holding the bedcovers up to her chin, a combination of fear, trauma and fatigue draining her of all life and emotion.

"If there's anything you need, you only have to call us. Take care of yourselves." He stood up and started to leave.

"Why did you care so much about me?" Jenna asked Abby softly.

"Because it's our job, and because I care," Abby replied.

"Who's going to look after me now?" she asked, her eyes heavy with sadness.

"You'll have plenty of people looking after you both. Here is my card." She handed one to each girl. "Now you have my number too. You'll be getting specialist help to get you through this and process what you've been through. But call me if you need me. Or even if you just want to talk, I don't mind, just ring me."

Jenna glanced at the card between her fingers, unsure how to react. She was struggling to accept that someone was showing a genuine interest in her for the very first time.

She licked her cracked lips as her mind raced to formulate something to say. "What's in it for you?"

Abby smiled. "There's nothing in it for me. I just care about what happens to you, that's all."

Jenna shrugged. "No one has ever said that to me before. Why should I believe you?"

Abby tilted her head at her. "Because there's always a first time."

Jenna's face began to soften with the slightest hint of happiness. She was still unsure how to react to something that had been missing for such a long time in her life: unconditional kindness.

WE HOPE YOU ENJOYED THIS BOOK

ALSO BY JAY NADAL

TIME TO DIE

(Book 1 in the DI Scott Baker series)

THE STOLEN GIRLS

(Book 2 in the DI Scott Baker series)

ONE DEADLY LESSON

(Book 3 in the DI Scott Baker series)

IN PLAIN SIGHT

(Book 4 in the DI Scott Baker series)

Printed in Great Britain
by Amazon

43273764R00148